I0610084

The Lodgers

By Annette Creswell

Outer Banks Publishing Group
Raleigh/Outer Banks

 Published in the United States of America by Outer Banks Publishing Group – Outer Banks/Raleigh.

www.outerbankspublishing.com

For information contact Outer Banks Publishing Group at

info@outerbankspublishing.com

Cover photo by PublicDomainArchive at Pixaby.com

FIRST EDITION – May 2021

Library of Congress Control Number: 2021936200

ISBN – 978-1-7367218-1-0
eISBN – 978-1-0057873-4-9

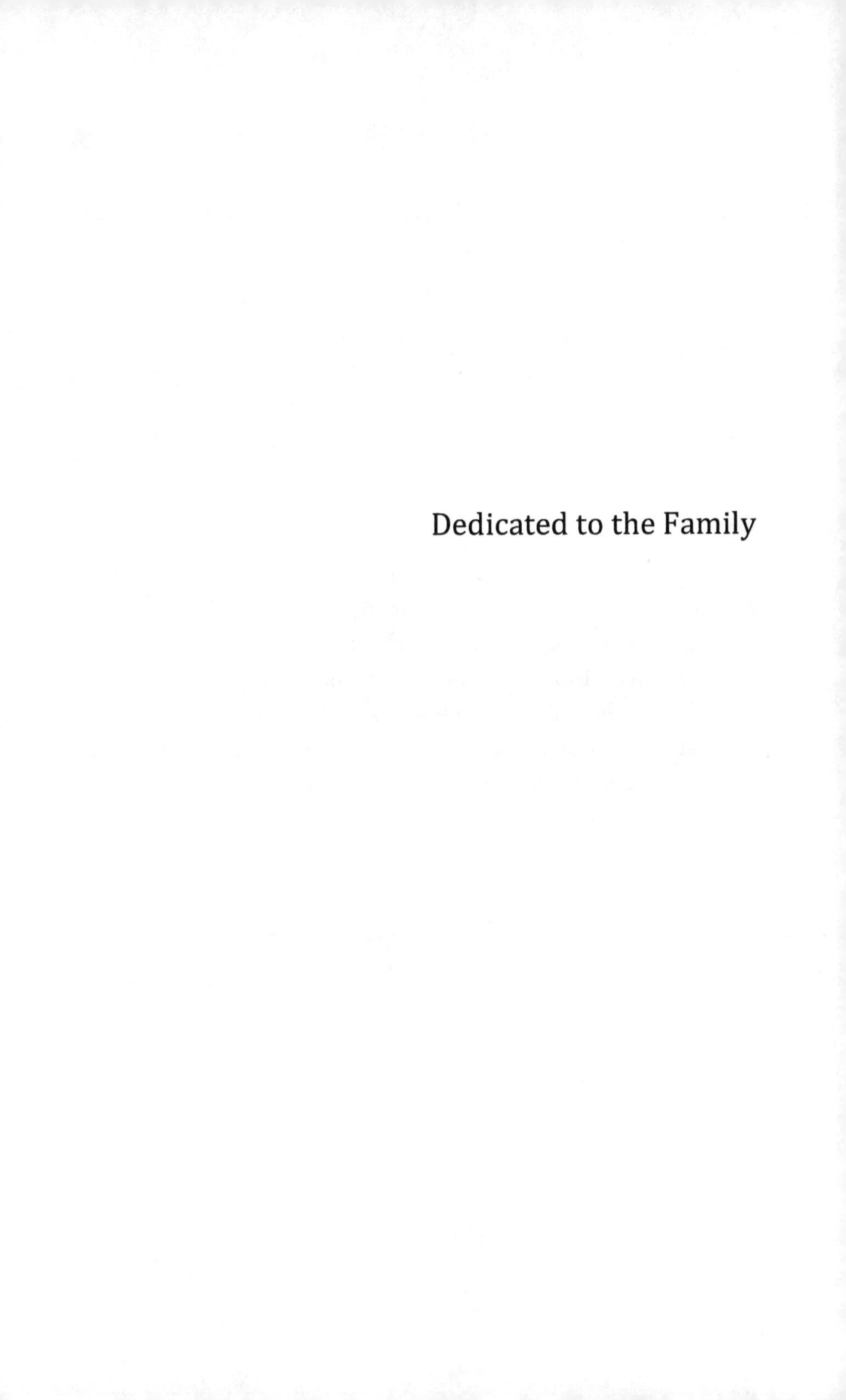

Dedicated to the Family

Acknowledgement

I wish to thank my wonderful agent Emerantia Parnall-Gilbert of Hawskspurr Productions for her friendship and invaluable assistance in bringing my novels to fruition.

My gratitude also extends to my publisher Anthony Policastro and all the dedicated team at Outer Banks Publishing Group.

Finally, a special thanks to Brett whose inspiration and encouragement resurrected my interest in writing.

Also by Annette Creswell

The Dark Before the Dawn

Just before the start of World War II, Peggy Davis, a London midwife, has a chance encounter with a stranger that changes her life forever.

When Peggy meets Charles, a wealthy lord as she boards a bus in front of Harrods department store, fate casts them together.

When Charles' wife, Diana, and first child die in childbirth, Peggy, and Charles are thrust into a relationship of happiness, sorrow and unexpected tragedy.

They ultimately marry, have a son and adopt an east end refugee boy from London.

What transpires is a web of family dramas a la Downton Abbey with lesbian relationships, Nazi sympathizers and family secrets revealed as Peggy attempts to navigate through her new life from midwife to lady of the manor.

Chapter One

Fresh tears spilled down Therese's cheeks as she read her mam's letter telling her how little Nessie was getting along with the reading. How she missed her family in Dublin but here she was in this desperate place in Brighton hiding away from all those sticky beak neighbours who would have pointed her out in the street.

"Oh, will you look at the brazen huzzy now, with her belly showing? A disgrace is all she is, giving herself to that Dougal feller with nary a wedding ring on the finger!"

And her mam, face red with the shame of it, would have hung her head and scuttled inside to get away from them all. Thank God her da had not known what had happened. He would have taken his fist or worse to Dougal, and anyone else who tried to besmirch his family's good name. The Gardai would have been called and da would have been put in the lock up for sure.

No, it was far better all round that she had taken the ferry that night to Holyhead, her mam telling everyone that Therese had gone to work at a fancy hotel in London.

"To be sure that Therese would land on her feet, always a one for a bit of the travelling. Sure, she will be the manageress as quick as you like" would then be the refrain.

Therese blew her nose and put away the letter, and then with nothing better to do, lay back down on her bed and pulled over the covers. She ran her hand over her stomach and all the worries of her predicament descended again.

Oh, God, what will I do? I can't go to that convent mam wanted me to go to and have some strangers take the baby. That would surely be too terrible! But would I have the courage to see that doctor abroad in Argyll Street? The one that girl told me about on the ferry over? I can't afford to keep the baby. I can hardly afford to keep myself. It was lucky that I had some money saved from those waitressing tips at the cafe in Dublin which was where I met Dougal.

Ah Dougal! She had noticed his red hair as soon as he had removed his cap and sat down, his blue eyes scanning the menu. He had asked what would she recommend for a starving docker like him? She had suggested the fish and chips, the special of the day.

When she had brought his plate over, she had whispered she had managed to sneak a few extra chips. He had beamed a grateful smile and gave her a wink, which had lifted her spirits, and she hoped that he would be a regular customer. This turned out to be the case and it was not long until he had asked her out to the Black Bull in Talbot Street. Over port and lemon for her and a pint for him she had been beguiled by those blue eyes and charming ways of the red headed docker sitting opposite her in the snug.

It was only a matter of weeks when Therese had found herself under his lithe freckled body. Whispering endearments in her ear, he had had his way with her. It had all been over in a matter of minutes leaving Therese sore and disappointed that the act of love was not what she had expected it to be.

Dougal had said as it was the first time for her she would not need to worry about falling pregnant. A fat lot he had known, thought Therese as she wiped fresh tears from her eyes. She did not want to marry someone deceitful like him, spinning tales about how he loved her so that he could have his jollies. No, she surely could do better than him and she wanted to see a bit of the world before she settled down.

Therese had not contacted him, nor had he contacted her, since she had confessed all to her mother. Having heard her bringing up her breakfast on more than one occasion, and the absence of the monthly rags on the line, her suspicions had been aroused. Through her tears, Therese had told her how her breasts were sore, the absence of the curse, and how she had given in to Dougal.

Brow pink with the intensity of the shock and anger, her mother had railed and ranted saying Therese was no better than she should be. She was like one of those sluts down at the wharf, spreading their legs to any Tom, Dick or Harry, and if her father ever heard about it there would be hell to pay! That Dougal would be made to walk her down the aisle, that is if a gun did not finish him off first. Make no mistake, her da would not have that sort of shame brought on the family!

Then, after the tirade and all recriminations had been spent and prayers to the Lord for his forgiveness had been offered, her mother, scarf over the head, had left Therese in charge of the little ones. She had scurried off down the lane to old mother Hobbs, the one to whom the women went when the unwanted pregnancies presented themselves.

There her mother was advised to put Therese in a bath as hot as she could stand while swallowing as much gin as she could. If this remedy did not work, she was to take the special tincture which Hobbs had made up.

So, with the advice and the tincture secreted close to her heart, Therese's mother flew back to the house and told her daughter how they were going to proceed. It was decided that they would wait until the afternoon after her da had eaten his lunch and gone back to work at the wharf and the little ones, down for their naps.

The bath took a long time to fill as many kettles had to boil, but at last it was ready, and Therese gingerly dipped her toe into the steamy water. It was much too hot so cold water had to be added. With tears cascading down her face, Therese eased herself in, while her mother stood by with the glass of gin. However, she had only managed to swallow half a glass when her head had dropped down into the water as a fainting spell had overtaken her. Her mother dropped the glass on the floor with the shock of it all. She heaved Therese up out of the water and, when she had come to, helped her out of the bath.

She was as red as a lobster and as unsteady as a drunkard as her mother wrapped her in a towel and helped her into her bed, now to be joined by Nessie and Donal who had been awoken by the shattering glass. They wanted to know why Therese was all red and talking funny like when their da had been at the pub too long, and why was she in the bed and not at the cafe?

"Mother of God, will you stop with the questions!" their mother had screamed.

"Therese is poorly, that's all. Now, for the love of the saints, will you go and play outside and give us some peace!"

Therese had stayed in bed until the next day and, apart from a terrible headache and a raging thirst, there was no sign of any miscarriage occurring. Therese's mother had rushed off to the cafe informing the proprietor that Therese was in bed with the flu and would not be in for a few days. Then, arriving back, it was time for the last resort: the special tincture of mother Hobbs! Poor Therese did not think she could bear any more of these treatments, none of which had had any effect whatsoever. Nevertheless, her mother was not to be deterred and, ensuring her daughter drank every last drop of the vile tasting liquid, sent prayers to St Jude, help of the hopeless, to help her and her daughter out of this terrible disaster!

However, St Jude had not been listening to any supplications that day, as Therese had spent most of the morning in the toilet, groaning with violent cramps as her bowels expelled their contents and her stomach followed suit. Therese's womb continued to hold fast the eight-week foetus. Her mother then decided the only course of action was for Therese to catch the ferry to England and get herself into one of the convents which took in unmarried mothers, adopting the babies out. She had heard that there was such a place in Brighton where Sally Collins had gone last year. It was run by the Sisters of Mercy.

Yes, she told Therese, that was where she was going, and they would invent a story to tell her da, Mr Jenkins at the cafe, and all the neighbours hereabouts. She would be going to work in a hotel over there to further her career. Then, when the coast was clear and she was no longer pregnant, she would return to Dublin and resume her life as though nothing had ever happened.

Therese listened to her mother but she had other ideas. She would go to Brighton but not to any convent. She would find herself somewhere to stay- a room would be all she would need and then she could decide for herself what her plan would be. She could easily write in her letters about life in the convent and there would be a Brighton postmark so nobody would be any the wiser. Also, she would tell her mother to send the mail to a post office box in Brighton, the nuns being strict about mail being sent to the girls at the convent.

As the voice of the rain diminished, leaving only the faulty guttering dripping resoundingly, Therese got up off the bed, went over to the table and sat on the chair. She opened the note pad, and taking the pen commenced to write:

Brighton
21st March 1950

Dear mam,

Thank you for your welcome letter. It has been raining cats and dogs.

Chapter Two

Irene could not concentrate on her crossword. When she became stumped at 11 across 4 down, she decided not to pursue it any longer, and instead readied herself for her visit to her sister. She went over to the mirror and swiped her lips with lipstick. Don't know why I bother, she thought, getting too old, wrinkles everywhere, and Lord knows where Judy is, nobody to impress there!

She shut the door and made her way downstairs passing by the sink and noticed the tap dripping-nobody taking any heed of the old faded, written sign DONT LEAVE TAP DRIPING. She went over and turned it off. Wasting water-nobody cares, been the same as long as I have lived here. You would think Mabel would have it fixed.

She passed her in the hall.

"Lovely day Irene. Are you visiting your sister then?"

"Oh, hello Mabel. Yes, I am."

"Has she improved at all?"

"No, not really I'm afraid. She just sits in the chair, with that vacant look on her face."

"Oh, I am sorry to hear that. But I suppose there are many like her, poor souls, with all the bombing that went on."

"Yes, I thank the good lord I was here in Brighton away from it."

"By the way," she added "The boiler in the bathroom needs seeing to. When I turned it on the other day it made a terrible noise. I thought it was going to explode in my face!"

Mabel patted her hair, eyebrows lifted.

"Oh, is that right? I'll see to it then."

"Well, better get on. Time waits for no man" she added anxious to get away from lodgers complaining about any more things which were in need of repair.

She bustled off in the direction of the basement where there were a couple of transsexual thespians ensconced. In her hey-day, Mabel had been in show business, performing in various vaudeville acts, singing and dancing and, according to rumours, Mabel had let the old queens stay there for a peppercorn rent.

Probably going to see those two in the basement, Irene thought to herself. Well, live and let live. That's my motto!

She approached the station and, after her ticket was purchased, boarded the train which would take half an hour on a private line directly to the Helingly asylum.

As she walked through the iron gate and up the path the mammoth building loomed ahead. Under the gunmetal sky it looked more foreboding than ever, and Irene put her head down and pulled her coat more firmly around her.

There were a few inmates walking around the grounds, some talking to themselves, others waving their arms, railing and ranting to an invisible presence only they could see. She went through to the reception and was told that her sister was in the recreation room.

As she walked along the corridor, she was suddenly accosted by an inmate who lunged at her and tried to poke her in the eye. Hearing her screams, an orderly came quickly to her aid and grabbed the patient, globs of molten abuse spewing from his mouth, as he was escorted back to the ward. I wish there was more security in here, thought Irene. A body is not safe.

She soon came to the room in which sat her sister with the same vacant look, but today she was rocking, pulling at her hair.

Irene pushed a chair over and sat down. She put her bag on the floor then patted her sister's hand.

"Judy, it's me Irene" she said "I've come to see you again."

No response came forth.

A nurse appeared and told Irene that today was not one of Judy's good days. Apparently, her mood had changed when a low flying plane had come over when she was sitting outside and all the bad memories had surfaced. That was the worst day of the blitz, when the Germans had rained terror on London. Buildings had been blown to smithereens while firemen tried to extinguish the multitudinous fires which had resulted. Judy had been in her parents' home which had taken a direct hit.

She was found unconscious under the broken body of her poor mother who had tried to shelter her daughter from the onslaught, while the remnants of her father's body had been recovered under pieces of masonry. Judy had been extricated from the ruins and transported by ambulance to the emergency department of the nearest hospital; the overworked nurses trying their best to quickly triage the increasing numbers of wounded being brought through the doors. She was taken straight to the theatre where her legs were saved but her mind was not. After spending two months in the hospital, she was moved to a facility better able to deal with the trauma she had experienced. This facility was Helingly asylum where she had been incarcerated for three years, with not a word uttered.

Judy previously had been a typist in a typing pool at Guardian insurance in London, and after some time had been promoted to secretary to one of the directors, Peter Hughson. However, it was not long until the boss/secretary relationship changed to something more personal as she found herself being slowly seduced by this married man. Initially, it had started as an invitation to lunch for a job well done, then progressed to a drink after work, dinners in out of the way restaurants, and finally a weekend in a country hotel. Judy knew what she was doing was wrong, but believed all that Peter had told her: he would soon be leaving his wife who did not understand him, and would then marry her.

The day when Peter had told her he was not leaving his wife was the day when the bomb had hit. Devastated, she had run out of the office in tears, jumped on a bus, and arrived home to her startled parents who wondered what had been the cause of their daughter's distress. They had not had long to wonder as it was then that they were both annihilated.

"Judy" said Irene again as she tried to enlist some kind of response from her sister but she continued on pulling her hair oblivious to everything around her.

"I don't think you will get much out of her today," said the nurse.

"When she is like this it takes a while before she calms down. She will be due for her injection soon. Why don't you take yourself off to the canteen and have a cup of tea and something to eat? Better than sitting here amongst all the bedlam."

Just as she finished speaking an inmate, who had been previously sitting on a chair, jumped and threw himself at the window cracking it in the process, while his screeches reverberated around the room. This brought two burly wardens who manhandled the patient and, after putting him into a strait jacket, carted him off to the isolation ward.

"Yes, that is a good idea nurse" said Irene obviously quite unsettled by the drama which had just unfolded.

"I think I will have a cuppa."

Patting her sister's head, she took her bag and headed off in the direction of the canteen.

"What'll you 'ave love?" asked the waitress as Irene approached the counter.

"Oh, a cup of tea please" replied Irene "And maybe a sandwich. What sort do you have?"

"There's cheese and pickle, or I can do you a spam and tomato if you like."

"Oh, let's see. I think I will take the cheese thank you" said Irene.

"Right, you are then ducks. Take a seat and I'll bring it to yer."

Irene found a table near a window which looked as though it had not seen a rag for years; the caked-on grime making it impossible to discern anything of substance outside.

The room was vast with high ceilings and Formica covered tables. The walls were painted a dirty shade of green, and the scuffed lino bore testament to the many feet which had traversed its surface over the years.

"Here we are, love, this will keep you going. Visiting someone are ya?" the waitress asked as she set Irene's dinner down on the table.

"Thank you" said Irene "Yes, I'm visiting my sister as a matter of fact."

"Oh, has she been in here long?"

"Yes, she has."

"How long?"

"Three years."

"Gawd, that long! Is she gettin' any better?"

"No, she isn't. She's asphasic."

"And what's asasic, when it's at home?"

"It's called asphasic" corrected Irene, "It means she doesn't speak."

With that Irene was aware of her eyes misting with tears and she took her handkerchief from her bag.

"There now lovey. Don't take on. I'm sure she'll get better. They're always coming up with new treatments and such like.

Irene wiped her eyes and took a sip of tea and wished this woman would go away and leave her in peace. Fortunately, this was what she did as she had noticed an elderly couple waiting at the counter.

"Well, better go. You enjoy your dinner," she said as she plodded off to take their order.

As Irene took a bite of the sandwich, the couple walked over and sat down at the table next to her.

"Well, Stanley" said the woman "It's good to sit down here and have a cuppa. I don't think I could have dealt with any more of that what they give our Doris. It's inhuman, that's what it is!"

"Now, Nelly, don't work yourself up again. They told us it's the best treatment. Nothing else has worked has it?" replied the man, presumably her husband.

"No, it hasn't. I just don't like the way it's done. Putting that rubber thing in her mouth and turning on the electric. It's like she were a criminal being killed in one of them chairs!"

Irene sat transfixed by the conversation taking place and hoped that Judy would not be subjected to such treatment. She had heard it was called electric shock therapy, and by what she was hearing it sounded quite barbaric.

The couple now occupied with tea and cake discontinued their conversation leaving Irene to her thoughts.

Please God, she prayed, as she took another bite of her sandwich, make Judy better so she can come and live with me at Mabel's where I can look after her. I can ask for that bigger room on the next floor now that Jimmy and his wife have moved on. Yes, that's a nice room. Has some light coming in, and Jimmy did a good job painting the walls that nice shade of cream. Better than my place. That brown wallpaper had seen better days and no mistake. Think I'll invest in a new rug. Makes all the difference, a nice colourful rug. Reminds me of the one I had in my room at Ranelagh house. Now that was nice. Persian I think it was. Yes, I did have it good there, but no use crying over spilt milk.

Irene had left home as a girl of sixteen. She had always wanted to be a nanny looking after the children of the gentry and living in a grand house in the country. This she had achieved when she was interviewed by lady Grimson of Ranelagh house in Sussex where she had been in charge of two children, Lucy and Henry. She had been with the family for many years but her problem with alcohol became her undoing leading to a shameful dismissal.

She had partaken of an alcoholic drink only occasionally on social occasions, but due to the worry about her sister's liaison with Peter Hughson, which she knew would end in tears, and her mother's ill health: she had been diagnosed with cancer of the pancreas, she had turned to the bottle for some comfort. She had been told by one of the nannies whom she used to meet at the park that alcohol was a great panacea for worries, having helped her aunt through a rough time when her husband had left her for another woman.

"Go one Irene" she had said.

"Give it a go."

So, with the children in tow, she had detoured to the grocers one afternoon and bought a cheap bottle of sherry telling the proprietor it was for the cook, as she had run out.

At first, it had helped her sleep and obliterated all the stress and anxiety but, as time went on, and she had procured more supplies, she found it was having the reverse effect, and she had lain awake in her bed watching the hands of the bedside clock move slowly around its face.

She also had the worry of being found out by the rest of the servants, especially the officious housekeeper, Mrs Danks, who always had her ear to the ground, not much escaping her notice.

However, Irene had managed to avoid her especially in the mornings when, bleary eyed, she had escaped to the nursery where she would ensconce herself with the children until the coast was clear. Also, she always ensured she had a good supply of peppermints to mask any offending odours which might emanate from her mouth.

As time went on she found she could not function if she did not have a drink, and when she heard the horrific news that her parents had both been killed and her sister severely injured that was the time she had really hit rock bottom. The parlourmaid, Pratt, had reported her key to the wine cupboard missing, and had subsequently discovered Irene in the act of stealing a vintage bottle of cabernet. She had been immediately summoned by her ladyship who, although sympathetic to her troubles, was told she could no longer be entrusted to care for the children. She had been summarily dismissed with advice to obtain immediate help for her alcoholism.

Shame- faced, bleary eyed, and with a blinding headache, she had left early the next morning with Tim the chauffeur who took her and her luggage to the station where she had boarded the train to Brighton.

On arrival, she had asked the stationmaster if he knew of a cheap lodging house nearby, and he had directed her to Mabel's, to which she had staggered. Dragging her suitcase along the footpath, the cacophony of seagulls which swooped and dived along the pier did nothing to quieten the throbbing in her head.

Finally she arrived at the drab, brown building and going through the gate she had discerned a Room to Let sign on the front window, a twitching of the lace curtain, and a glimpse of red hair. This had belonged to Mabel who had opened the door and ushered her in through the gloomy interior: the brown walls seeming to jeer at her as she was led up the stairs.

Thirty bob had been the sum which Mabel had demanded from her, commenting that she could get more but she could see that Irene had a ladylike demeanour underneath her dishevelled appearance. She could see that this new lodger had clearly been someone who had fallen on hard times.

"Want another cuppa?" asked the waitress bringing Irene out of her reverie.

"Pardon? Oh no, thank you," said Irene.

It was for her dear departed parents, Judy, and herself, that she looked down into the cup of the unfinished, unmilked tea then, taking her bag, she walked off to farewell her sister.

As the train transported Irene back from Helingly, her mind licked around the events of her visit. It had again been emotionally draining and seemed to be becoming more so as the time went on. She had managed to speak with Judy's doctor, Professor Mumford, before she left the facility. They had crossed paths as Irene had left the canteen on her way to farewelling her sister. He had told her that in his opinion shock therapy might be the best treatment for Judy. He had said that they were having much success in improving cases such as Judy's, however he felt he had to mention that in rare cases, it might bring on violent tendencies in some people. Irene was quite taken aback by this. She wanted her sister to be able to talk again but was terrified by the idea of the shock therapy, the barbarism of it, and the fact that it could turn her violent! Was that a risk she was willing to take? Could she live with herself if things went wrong and Judy was left in a far worse state than she was now, or, heaven forbid, even dead? It did not bear thinking about.

The train drew into the station and Irene sighing, took her bag, alighted and commenced her walk up the hill to her lodgings as rain clouds gathered threatening to release their cargo at any minute. She hurried along, hot with haste, as she had not bothered to bring her umbrella and just made it when the first drops of rain appeared.

As she passed by Mabel's room, she heard laughter and singing coming from within. Mabel must have one of the queens in for a sing-along thought Irene. She certainly spends a lot of time with them. Think she would have more things to do with her time, like fixing that dripping tap for instance, and that light which always goes out when a body is walking up the stairs in the dark.

As she mounted the first stair, Mabel's door opened and out flounced one of the queens resplendent in a lurid red frock with matching lips and nails.

"Evening" she said to Irene.

"Good evening," she replied.

"Been out have you?" she asked.

"Yes I have. Just this minute got in."

"Been having a sing song with Mabel" she offered.

"Just popping down the road for some more ciggies."

"Oh yes?"

"Want to come and join us? That woman likes to party."

"Oh no, I don't think so. I'm rather tired. Think I'll be having an early night, thanks all the same."

"Suit yourself," she replied over her shoulder mincing out the door.

Irene reached her room and put her bag on the chest of drawers, then passing by the mirror, noticed her reflection. It was of a tired, haggard looking individual. Must take more care of myself, should go and get a haircut, at least a tidy up. Letting myself go these days what with the worry of Judy. Tomorrow have to go to the AA meeting. Must not let that slip. Been on the wagon for three years now. Haven't had a drop. Downstairs she could hear the piano still being played and she hoped they would soon finish soon as Mabel was known to be fond of the all nighters when she had the chance!

She was about to boil the kettle and make herself something for tea when her thoughts turned to poor Arthur Curtis on the next floor. She had not been to see him for a few days and decided his company would be just what she needed after that stressful visit at Helingly. Much rather spend time with him than that lot downstairs-larking about, on the drink.

She locked the door and, with her spirits lifted, made her way up the creaking stairs carefully avoiding the pieces of threadbare carpet which always threatened to trip her up.

"Hello, hello, Arthur, are you there?" she said knocking on the door. She waited for a couple of minutes as she knew Arthur's movements were getting slower these days. He suffered from a bad knee which had resulted when a piece of Flanders shrapnel had embedded itself, and the tentacles of rheumatism were slowly entangling themselves around his joints.

The door opened a fraction to reveal Arthur's wrinkled face.

"Oh, hello Irene," he said opening the door wider.

"Hello Arthur. Is this a good time to see you? I hope you weren't having a nap or anything?"

"No, no, my good woman. Come in, come in."

Irene did as she was bid and followed Arthur as he shuffled into the room. It was neat and tidy as Arthur had been a major and everything had to be ship-shape. His shoes he kept polished to a fine shine and his hair always had a sharp part along the side.

"Have a seat, my dear," said Arthur gesturing with his stick to an easy chair covered with a brown woollen blanket.

"No, no, that is your chair Arthur. You sit on it. I will take the other one," protested Irene.

"Oh, are you sure? Well, if you don't mind. This wretched knee has been playing up lately" he said as he reclaimed the chair, sitting down heavily and putting his stick on the floor beside him.

Irene pulled the other chair closer to Arthur then sat down.

"Sorry to hear you're not doing so well. You know, it's probably the weather. I remember my uncle's arthritis used to worry him when it became a bit damp."

"Now" she added leaning over and patting his hand "How about I make us a nice cup of tea?"

"Oh, yes, that would be lovely, thank you Irene. You know where everything is."

Irene went to the sink, filled the kettle and put it on the hotplate to boil, then assembled the cups and saucers.

She came and sat down again.

"Well, it's good to see you. How have you been, and how is your sister?" asked Arthur.

Irene, fingers worrying her necklace, replied.

"Oh, I'm fair to middling I suppose Arthur, but Judy isn't so well. I've just come from visiting her. She had one of her turns the other day. Got scared of a plane when she was sitting outside. When I saw her, she was rocking back and forth and pulling her hair. The nurse said when she's like that it takes a few days for her to settle down."

"Oh, dear. I'm so sorry. That is bad."

"Yes, I hate seeing her like that. I had a chance to speak to her doctor while I was there."

She heard the kettle had boiled and walked over to make the tea.

"And what did he say?" called Arthur.

Irene dropped three spoonfuls of tea into the pot and poured in the water.

"Well," she responded, "He seemed to think that shock therapy might be useful."

She poured the tea into the cups and brought them over.

"There should be a few biscuits in the tin if you would like some." said Arthur.

"Oh, alright, thank you. Would you like one?" asked Irene walking over and opening the tin to find four shortbread biscuits lurking inside.

"Yes, I think I would fancy one with the tea."

She put two on a plate and brought it over then sat down again.

"You were saying about the shock treatment" said Arthur taking his cup and dunking the biscuit into his tea.

"Oh, yes. Well, he said it might work for Judy but in some cases, there was a risk of violent behaviour. I'm worried about that aspect and also the treatment itself. I overheard some people at the asylum talking about what is involved. Apparently, their daughter had undergone it and it sounded quite barbaric. They put some sort of rubber in their mouths and then turn on the electricity!"

Arthur saw the worried look on his visitor's face.

"Now, I'm sure it's not as bad as it seems," he said.

"If there is a chance of curing Judy, then that is the way to go. It is hard I know, but the risks have to be weighed up, and you must abide by the opinions of the professionals. After all, they are the ones with the experience, aren't they?"

Irene bit into her biscuit and looked down at the crumbs of shortbread on her skirt. She noticed one of the threads had pulled and determined to repair it when she went home.

"Yes, I suppose you're right. She deserves a chance to get better. She's been in that place for so long with no quality of life. I would love it if she improved enough to come and live here with me."

Arthur raised his eyebrows then took Irene's hand.

"Then you must agree to the treatment, my dear. What is the saying? Nothing ventured, nothing gained?"

Irene managed a wan smile and agreed with this wise man sitting opposite her.

"Yes, that is the saying, and I suppose I must give her a chance."

"That's the spirit, my dear. Now, what other news? Have you seen anything lately of the young lady downstairs?"

"You mean, Therese? No, as a matter of fact I haven't. She seems to keep to herself. Poor little thing. I do feel sorry for her closeted in this place away from her family. I will look in on her tomorrow and see how she is."

"Give her my best wishes if you do see her," said Arthur.

"I will."

Irene took a sip of her tea then asked.

"Have you heard from the family lately?"

"Yes, as a matter of fact. I received a letter from Ben."

Ben was Arthur's grandson who was in the hospitality industry. After he left school, he earned some money working at various bars, now he was working his way up the ladder at the Bournemouth hotel. He was now the bar and lounge manager with hopes of becoming the food and beverage manager in a few years' time.

Arthur was understandably proud of Ben, his only grandchild as, to the mortification of Arthur, Ben's father, Ned, had been court martialled and shot for desertion at Tobruk. His wife, Moira had never recovered from the shock of that day when she was found by her son slumped over the kitchen table the tear soaked telegram lying at her feet.

It was only a matter of months when, overcome with depression, while Ben was at school, she had ended her life in the mouth of the gas oven in the Camden family home. Ned's sister, Betty who had not been able to have children had then stepped in and raised Ben until he was old enough to be independent. However, her husband Brian, a property developer with more money than compassion, had never been agreeable to the arrangement, and there were many rows some resulting in physical violence towards his wife as he thought she was devoting too much time to Ben and not enough to him. She had secretly put money away to pay for some therapy for Ben as she knew how her husband would react.

"Don't see why we should be looking after him. Can't he live with his Grandfather?" He had said when Ben had moved into the residence at Chelsea.

"And what's this about him wanting to work in pubs like a serving wench? He's nothing but a sissy. And you don't help, pandering to his every whim, turning him into a mummy's boy, a milksop! Any wonder his old man got the bullet for being soft. Like father, like son. The apple doesn't fall far from the tree!"

The whisky sodden words spat out at his wife would always have the desired effect, goading her on until there was a full-scale argument. This would either end in her fleeing to the bedroom in tears or feeling the force of his fists as she cowered in a corner meekly trying to defend herself against the onslaught.

Fortunately, Ben was not witness to these episodes as Betty tried to keep the peace when he was home. He suspected his uncle was abusing his aunt but felt powerless to do anything. Many a night he would lie in bed with his fingers in his ears and the blanket pulled over his head to extinguish the noise of the fights taking place downstairs. He longed for the day when he could earn some money, leave and live by himself in peace.

As the marriage deteriorated, Brian had ultimately left Betty for a girl old enough to be his daughter, so Arthur had said. He also had said that it was good riddance to him. Betty was too good for a bounder like that, he never did like the way he treated his daughter. He had suspicions that he was even hitting her, as more than once Betty had presented with bruises to her face and arms, and she, blaming the furniture with which she had collided. She had never mentioned to Arthur of her husband's feelings towards Ben as she knew it would be too painful for him to bear.

Arthur was still trying to come to terms with the whole sorry, tragic business. However, having ruminated about things, he knew that his son had always had a nervous disposition which would not have been conducive in the maelstrom of war.

Hunkered down, quivering in a trench, the deafening noise of the cannons penetrating his brain, and the hot Libyan sand turning his tears into mud, his nerves would have been at breaking point. He also had heard that the German, field Marshall, Rommel was unstoppable, and this fact alone would have added to his anxiety.

Poor Ned always had a nervous disposition, he would tell anyone who knew the truth of his demise. However, not many people were aware, as the family decided to keep it a secret, saying that Ned had been one of the many who had fallen in the service to their country.

After he and others like him were shot at dawn by firing squad, their bodies had been transported, not to the verdant fields of England, but to the hot sandy soil of a Libyan military cemetery.

Betty had tried to have Ned's remains brought back. She had even enlisted the help of Arthur as he had contacts in the army, but to no avail. The authorities could not be dissuaded: the rules were there and were not to be broken on any account. Betty had promised herself that somehow, one day, she would travel to her brother's resting place in that foreign land and put on his grave a sprig of the English cow parsley he so used to love.

"Is Ben still at that hotel?" asked Irene.

"Yes, he is, and he's doing very nicely for himself. Working his way up the ladder," replied Arthur.

“I’m so pleased. Has he met anyone special? I remember you saying he had his eye on that girl who was on the reception.”

“Oh, I don’t think that ever came to anything. Ben told me she was just playing the field. Not interested in settling down. I don’t think he is about to settle down either between you and me.

“Well, he is only young and there are lots more fish in the sea, as they say,” replied Irene glancing at her watch.

“Is that the time? I must be going. I didn’t realise it was that late. I have overstayed my welcome.”

“No, no, not at all Irene. It was lovely to have some company. They do say that time flies when you are having fun!”

“Yes, so they do. Well, goodbye Arthur. Take care of yourself,” Irene said standing up and walking to the door.

“Goodbye my dear,” Arthur said as he hauled himself out of the chair.

“Stay there, Arthur. I can see myself out.”

To the sound of Arthur’s voice telling her to come and visit him soon, Irene wended her way back to her room where, over a boiled egg and a slice of toast, she ruminated over the events of the day.

Chapter Three

After the torrential downpour of the previous night, shafts of sunlight now stole their way into Therese's room as she lay in her bed. Her eyes alighted on the letter written to her mother and she determined to post it this morning on her way out. The letter had contained sketchy accounts of life in the convent, especially descriptions of the imaginary pregnant girls whom she had befriended. The lies she was telling were anathema to her, but she hoped God would forgive her in the fullness of time.

During the night, after much soul searching, praying and deliberation, and before all courage was lost, Therese had decided she would call on that doctor about whom she had heard. She felt it was worth having another opinion about her options, and an opinion from a medical doctor made her feel somewhat reassured, albeit a little anxious about what he might have to tell her.

She got up, washed her face in the sink, brushed her auburn hair one hundred times as her mother had instructed, then pulled on her red jumper and an old skirt which she unearthed in the bottom of the drawer. As she had not worn it for a while, she was astounded to find it was now feeling a little tight around the waist. She undid the button on the side and felt immediately more comfortable.

Still suffering from occasional bouts of morning sickness, Therese did not feel like eating much for breakfast so decided to have a couple of bites of an apple which had been sulking in the dish for over a week.

Biting into it and discarding a bruised part of the skin, she cast her mind over the projects which had to be undergone today.

Firstly, the doctor, and then she had to see about securing some class of employment as her meagre savings were dwindling by the day. There were things to buy: food, clothes for herself (she could not wear this skirt for much longer) and if she was going to keep the baby that would be a big expense. She would breastfeed as long as she could to save buying bottles of formula, but even then there would be other things. Her mother was always railing about how much children cost.

The core of the apple was now all that was left, so Therese placed it in the rubbish bin then, taking her tube of lipstick off the chest of drawers went to the mirror and changed her pale lips into a bright shade of pink. Nearly satisfied with her appearance she closed the door and commenced walking down the stairs.

"Oh, hello Therese" exclaimed Irene shutting the door behind her.

"I was going to call and see how you were getting along."

"Oh, Irene, hello. I'm not too bad. I was just going out."

"Well, so am I. We can walk together. Which way are you going?" she asked as they both walked down the stairs to the front door.

Therese did not want Irene to know that she was on her way to the doctor around in Argyll Street as she had heard he was known to have a reputation of relieving girls of their maternal problems.

"Oh, I have to do some shopping" Therese said as another lie increased the tally.

"Well, I am catching the next bus, so we can walk down to the stop."

"Alright."

As they walked, Irene noticed how preoccupied her companion seemed, unresponsive to Irene's conversation. However, she was also pleased that Therese did not ask where she was going; the AA was not the place she would want anyone to know she was attending.

When they arrived at the destination, Irene patted Therese on the arm and told her if there was anything she could do to help just to let her know. Therese thanked her then went on her way straight into the first shop she came to which happened to be the butchers.

She skulked around at the counter, meanwhile looking through the window to see if the bus had arrived to take her neighbour away. The butcher came across and asked what she would like and, feigning the excuse of having forgotten her purse, she dashed outside just as the number 40 bus had pulled away from the kerb.

She crossed the road and continued walking looking at street names as she went but Argyll Street was not manifesting. I will have to ask someone for directions, she thought. I can't walk around here forever. Just then an elderly woman came around the corner carrying a string bag bursting with groceries.

"Oh, excuse me," said Therese as the woman came closer.

"Yes, dear, can I help you?"

"Yes, could you please tell me where Argyll Street is?"

The woman's brow furrowed.

"Argyll Street you say?"

"Yes, do you know where it is?"

"Well, I think you have come too far. You will have to go back to the park and turn left, then at the post box you turn right, or is it left? Oh, sorry dear, I can't remember!"

"Oh, well, I think I will find it, thank you" replied Therese to the retreating back of the woman.

With the directions committed to memory, and with the hope of success, Therese set off again and finally, after taking a few wrong turns, found Argyll Street and the doctor's surgery lurking behind a hedge. Nervously she opened the creaky gate, then knocked on the door which was opened by an officious receptionist who asked did she have an appointment?

The answer being no, Therese was grudgingly told to come and sit in the waiting room and wait for the doctor to see her. She was also told that it might take some time as usually the doctor only saw people with appointments.

Therese sat down and looked around the room. There were signs on the wall warning about the dangers of spitting in public which may result in spreading TB, and also the symptoms of gonorrohea and venereal disease. The latter accompanied by confronting images from which Therese had to avert her eyes.

She found her anxiety increasing as she was now worried that she could have these terrible diseases. Surely Dougal would not have given her such things, she was telling herself. It was bad enough that she was pregnant. Now here was something else to be concerned about! She started to say the rosary to calm her nerves, and was halfway through when a woman, in a state of extreme distress, emerged from the doctor's room. She staggered past Therese and, with a handkerchief to her mouth, left the surgery.

"Doctor will see you now" announced the receptionist as she stopped clacking on the typewriter.

Anxiously, Therese went into the inner sanctum.

"And what brings you here today, Mrs or is it Miss?" asked the presence at the other side of the desk as he looked at Therese's left hand trying to spot anything resembling a wedding ring.

"Oh, it's Miss, doctor" Therese tremulously replied.

"Miss who?" asked the doctor.

"Miss O'Brien, Therese O'Brien."

The doctor wrote this down.

"And why are you here today?"

With downcast eyes and sweaty hands clasped she answered.

"Well, you see doctor, I'm expecting."

"You mean you are pregnant?"

"Yes, that's right."

"And what do you propose doing about this state of affairs?"

"Well, to be sure, I don't know what to do. Sometimes I think I will keep it and other times I think I won't be able to. It costs money to bring up a baby so my mam always says. She thinks I am away in the convent with the nuns organizing an adoption."

The doctor continued to write then settling back in his chair, hands entwined, said.

"Well, depending how far along you are, you have the option of aborting. Do you know how many weeks you are now?"

"I think I am about eight weeks, doctor."

"Very good. Now, I have to examine you to ascertain if your estimate is correct. You can go behind here" he said pointing to the screen.

"Just take off your panties and leave everything else on" he advised.

Therese went behind the screen and did as she was instructed.

"Now" said the doctor "Get up onto the bed."

He came over, told her to open her legs and relax, then inserted the speculum.

Therese was too anxious to relax and was finding the whole process extremely uncomfortable and nerve wracking. As the doctor poked about she tried concentrating on the ceiling. She noticed a stain which looked like the shape of Tasmania. Now Australia was a country which she would like to visit. All those kangaroos and cuddly koala bears, but then there were all those creatures which could kill you too! Funnel web spiders, sharks and snakes! At least Ireland did not have any of those slithering around in the grass!

"All done," said the doctor "Get dressed and we will discuss your options" said the doctor going over to the desk.

Therese, transported back from the antipodes and glad that the ordeal was over, got up off the bed and, after putting on her underwear, went and sat down on the chair.

"Well, your estimation was correct. You are eight weeks pregnant which means you would be able to have an abortion, so you must make a quick decision. Another week and it becomes more complicated and more risky."

"And what if I decide to keep it? Would the government give me any money to help me out?" asked Therese hopefully.

"Government give you money?" he spluttered, "You must be joking!"

"No, my dear girl. The best you could hope for is to go to one of those charity refuges that cater for unmarried mothers with babies. I think there is one not far from here called Clark's House. You could stay there until your baby is born, but they only give you six weeks after that to decide if you want to keep the child or have it adopted."

Therese's face fell as she digested everything the doctor was telling her. It sounded like her choices were limited. Perhaps she should have heeded her mother's advice and taken herself to that convent after all.

The doctor pushed his chair back.

"Think carefully about your options, but if you decide to have the abortion you must do it by the end of next week.

And ensure you make an appointment. I am only available on Wednesday evenings at 7.00pm and the fee will be two guineas."

Then he added.

"I would appreciate your discretion. Do not tell anyone you are coming here. Everything must be kept confidential, you understand? We both don't want to end up in jail now do we? Oh, and bring plenty of sanitary towels with you in case there is some haemorrhaging."

Weighed down with these parting words and all that had transpired, Therese reeled blindly out of the surgery and onto the street. Her vision blurred with tears and her mind with worry, she desperately tried to recall which way she had come.

As she commenced walking, large drops of rain now fell from the clouds which had been gathering since the morning. She hurried on, her hair becoming more soaked and matted, while drips of water slid down the back of her neck. Was it the next street where I turned right, she wondered, as a car speeding past sent a spray of water all over her dress.

"Oh, Mother of God!" she wailed looking down at her mud splattered legs. She hurried on and, turning the corner, a cafe materialised. She lurched through the door and sat down at the nearest table, so glad to be out of the rain.

"You do look like a drowned rat!" said the waitress as she came over pencil and pad in hand poised to take her order.

"What will you be wanting?"

"Oh, just a cup of tea please" replied Therese mentally calculating if she could afford it as there was still food to be bought. The money she had saved from her previous job was earmarked for emergencies and now looked as though it would go to that doctor in Argyll Street.

"Right, you are then, dearie. You had better go into the lavatory and dry yourself off a bit before you catch your death. It's just over there on your left."

Therese found the lavatory just in time as it had been a while since her bladder had opened. Sitting on the seat she contemplated her situation: her pregnancy becoming more advanced as the seconds ticked on, the deadline for the abortion becoming more urgent, and her state of unemployment. Mary and Joseph, it was all too much! She pulled the chain, then taking some paper attempted to dry her soaked hair and clean some of the mud off her legs. To be sure I am a wreck, she said to the cracked mirror above the basin. That Dougal or anyone else wouldn't be chasing after me now! How can I look for some class of job in this condition?

The pot of tea was on the table when she returned and the waitress was desultorily giving the Formica tables a wipe with a rag.

She came over to Therese who was now being restored to some semblance of calm by the restorative tea.

"Bet that tea is warming the cockles of your heart" she said looking into the sugar bowl to assess the level.

"Oh, it is to be sure."

"Irish, are you?"

"Yes, I am."

"On holiday are you?"

"Oh no, not exactly," she replied eyes cast down, fingering the saucer.

Then the dam burst as all the pent-up emotion of the morning burst forth and she cried like her heart would break.

"There now. Things can't be that bad" said the waitress now sitting herself down at the table.

"They are" Therese managed to say through bouts of sobbing.

"I'm pregnant, and don't what to do. I'm supposed to be away in the convent where my mam thinks I am, but I'm in a room in an awful old boarding house, and I'm nearly broke because I haven't got a job, and I was going to look for a job today after I'd seen this doctor, but now I'm all wet and, and, I look a wreck."

The words cascaded from her lips in between the sobs which were racking her body.

The waitress concerned with Therese's distress patted her hand.

"Well, don't you worry about paying for the tea then love, it's on the house."

Taking her handkerchief from her bag, she wiped her eyes and blew her nose.

"Oh, tthank you" she stuttered.

"But won't you be in trouble with your boss?"

"Oh, he's not in today, and what he doesn't know won't hurt him" the waitress said with a finger to the side of her nose.

Just then the door opened, and two workmen plodded in. They sat down and looked at the menu.

"Be back in a minute, love. I better take their order. You just sit quietly and drink your tea."

She walked over.

"What can I get you?" she asked.

"A couple of your pork pies, and two teas thanks love" said one of the men.

Therese's stomach rumbled at the mention of the pies as her appetite was now returning and time had elapsed since the consumption of the breakfast apple. She tried to take her mind away from her hunger by spooning more sugar into the tea and looking at the dismal scene outside the window. Just as dismal as my life, she thought. Oh, Mother of God, tell me what to do!

The waitress having delivered the pies and tea to the men returned to Therese. Sitting down she said.

"So, you were saying you used to work in a cafe over in Ireland?"

"Yes" Therese replied turning her tear-stained face towards the waitress

"And I was good at it too. Used to get tips from the customers."

"Did you now?"

"My name's Mavis, by the way."

"I'm Therese, Therese O'Brien."

"Well, Therese, I have been thinking I might have a job for you. My friend, Dot is the manageress at that cafe down on the pier and she was telling me they are shorthanded at the moment. Mind, it wouldn't pay much, and I don't know how long they would be wanting you, but at least it would tide you over until something better comes along."

"Oh, really?" Oh, but that would be grand!"

"Well, at least it would solve one problem, but I can't give you much help with the other."

"Oh, I know. I have to decide soon one way or the other, but it's all so hard."

"Well, don't go doing anything stupid lovey. Just think everything over carefully and get yourself down to the pier straight away. Ask for Dot and tell her Mavis sent you, and if she doesn't take you on, tell her she will have me to answer to and no mistake!"

Therese went to go but a sick feeling came over her and she slid to the floor in a faint.

Mavis flew over and the men, pies abandoned, went to her aid. They hauled her up and back onto the chair.

"Sorry about that" whispered Therese as she came to.

"That's alright lovey. You just sit there until you feel better. I don't suppose you have eaten much today have you?" queried Mavis.

"No, I just had an apple this morning."

"Well, stay put and old Mavis will rustle you up a sandwich."

It was after a cheese sandwich and another cup of well sugared tea, that Therese found herself in the company of the two burly workmen as they escorted her down the street and pointed her in the direction of the Brighton pier.

Chapter Four

Irene slunk through the door her ears assailed by the familiar refrain of one of the longstanding members: "I am Denis and I am an alcoholic." She quickly took her place in one of the vacant chairs apologising to all for her late arrival. This had been due to a visit to the hairdresser for her much-needed trim. As there had been no appointment made, she had been forced to wait and read the dog eared magazines which, apart from being out of date, seemed to contain nothing more than scantily clad women and salacious gossip about film stars! Not to her taste at all. Should have brought my book, she thought as she turned another page to be confronted with another pair of partially clad breasts. Finally the hairdresser called her over to the chair and after covering her with the cape asked what style of cut she would like.

"Oh, nothing fancy. Just a trim thank you" Irene replied.

"You have a few split ends" said the girl taking up strands of Irene's hair.

"Yes, I suppose I do. It's a while since I have had it cut."

"Would you like it washed first?"

"Oh, well if it doesn't take too long. I have to be somewhere shortly."

"It shouldn't take too long."

"Well, alright then."

Irene was escorted to the basin and the girl commenced to wash her hair.

She heard the door open and a woman walking in.

"Be back in a minute" said the girl to Irene as she went over to talk to the customer, leaving Irene with her wet head tilted back over the basin.

The girl came back after settling the new customer in one of the chairs.

"Sorry about that. That is my 11 o'clock."

She continued to wash Irene's hair asking her was she going somewhere nice later to which Irene replied.

"Nowhere special. I just needed my hair trimmed." She wished that hairdressers would not always ask questions and indulge in chit chat. She hated it. All she wanted was to sit and have her hair fixed without all the blah, blah which seemed to be the want of all hairdressers. As if I'm telling her the AA meeting is my somewhere special! What a laugh that would be!

By the time the other customer was attended to and Irene's cut was administered, she knew she would be late for the meeting. This she also hated as all eyes would be on the latecomer, making her feel more anxious than she usually was when attending these meetings even after all this time. She looked in the mirror and found that she rather liked her hair cut, then giving her lips a swipe of lipstick paid the bill and hurriedly left the salon.

Denis, the new member, red faced, sat down relieved that his courage had not deserted him. It took a lot to come before strangers and admit that you are an alcoholic. Irene remembered that first day when she had come to this place. It had been the hardest thing she had ever had to say in public: "I am Irene, and I am an alcoholic." However, as hard as it had been, she knew it had saved her from the depravity into which she had been quickly tumbling, with death being the probable outcome.

The second night at Mabel's saw her in the bar at the Brighton hotel where she had tried to drown her sorrows in port. She was eventually escorted off the premises when the barman noticed her speech becoming more slurred and the front of her dress more stained. Mabel had hauled her into bed with severe admonishments, but nothing was a warning, and she continued on the path to perdition.

She went further afield, trying out bars in Hove where she knew she would not meet anyone who knew her. There were times when the milkman bore witness to the dishevelled woman trying to put her key into the lock of the brown lodging house in the early hours of the morning.

However, one morning she did not return to her room at all, as she had been taken by ambulance, siren blaring, to the Brighton hospital. Naked and unconscious, her face bruised and bleeding she had been found by one of the maids in the Excelsior Hotel. There was no sign of the perpetrator and after regaining consciousness, to the questioning of the Police, Irene had said she had no memory of the man she had been with, nor of how she came to be in the Hotel.

After tests had been conducted, she was made aware that to her horror, rape had occurred! She decided with tears of humiliation and despair, in that hospital bed, she had hit rock bottom and would now seek urgent help for her problem. A social worker was called to her bedside and she was given the name and address of Alcoholics Anonymous.

So here she was at another meeting which was now winding up, all the group therapy concluded, and the tea and biscuits consumed. All that remained was the plate to be handed around so donations could be placed for the upkeep of the hall.

"How are you, Irene?" asked Robert as they were leaving. He was an old acquaintance who was in the Police Force and whose wife had died a few years ago.

"Oh, not too bad thanks, Robert, how are you? I haven't seen you for ages." she replied.

"I've been living in Chester for a while. Had a posting there."

"Oh, I see. Well, it's good to see you again."

He asked.

"Are you still living at that lodging house?"

"Yes, still there. I've been there so long I don't think I could be bothered moving anywhere else."

They were now on the street and the wind had picked up blowing the leaves around their feet.

"Are you going straight back there now?" He enquired.

"Oh, I suppose so. I don't have any other plans."

"Well, we could go for an early tea if you like. There is a little cafe around the corner. It does good fish and chips."

Irene hesitated, then thought, oh what the heck, might as well go. Better than going back to my room like I usually do.

“That would be lovely. I rather feel like some fish and chips.”

“Good” said Robert adding.

“Your hair looks different.”

“I had it cut.”

“It suits you.”

“Oh, thank you, I only had a trim.” She replied, quite chuffed with his compliment.

They walked on to the cafe and over fish and chips splashed with vinegar Irene found to her surprise that she was enjoying the company of someone other than her fellow lodgers and was also pleased she had applied that coat of lipstick earlier. She remembered her former employer, lady Grimson, saying, a lady should never be seen in public with naked lips!

Chapter Five

It was now Tuesday, and Therese was in a state trying to decide if she would go ahead with the abortion tomorrow. She had been offered the job at the cafe on the pier, after telling the manageress her friend Mavis had sent her. It was not going to pay much but as beggars cannot be choosers, she thought it would be better than nothing, which was all she had at the moment. Oh God, how can I have this baby? How can I support it here on my own? Who is going to look after it when I have to go to work? The worrisome thoughts churned around and around her head until she finally came to a decision.

Wrapping a cardigan around her shoulders, Therese poked her head out of the door and, seeing the coast was clear, made her way down the stairs to the telephone which was outside the landlady's door. Checking there was still nobody about, with trembling fingers she dialled the number.

"Dr Wilson's surgery, Madge speaking," intoned the receptionist.

"Hello" squeaked Therese "I need to make an appointment to see the doctor tomorrow night at 7.00pm."

"I'm afraid doctor has another appointment scheduled at that time. He is available the following week if that is suitable." replied the receptionist.

"Oh, no," cried Therese.

"Please, I have to come tomorrow. It's urgent. The doctor told me I couldn't leave it for another week."

"Well, you should have made an appointment sooner then." She answered censoriously.

"What was your name?"

"It's O'Brien, Therese O'Brien."

By now, Therese was suffused with despair, thinking that she had left it too late and would not be able to have the abortion after all. The tears which had been threatening, now burst their banks and rolled down her cheeks onto the telephone.

Mabel's door opened.

Therese put her head down so Mabel could not see her distress and prayed to all the saints that her conversation had not been overheard.

"Hello, are you still there?" queried Madge.

"Ye, yes" stuttered Therese wishing Mabel would go away as at that minute she had decided to swipe a duster over the skirting boards obviously trying to listen in to the call.

"I have just spoken to the doctor. I had to interrupt his consultation with a patient. You are fortunate that he will see you tomorrow night. However, you will have to be here at 7.30."

"Oh, thank you" cried Therese "I'll be there."

"Very well. Remember to bring plenty of sanitary towels as doctor instructed and it would be advisable if you have someone take you home. Remember, 7.30 sharp and no later."

Therese put down the telephone and was not sure if the feelings she felt were of relief or terror.

"Are you alright dear?" asked Mabel coming over duster in hand, noticing Therese's tear splotched face,

"Oh, yes. I just had some bad news that's all."

"Oh, what happened? Is it your family?"

Therese thought fast.

"Yes, it's my little brother. He's sick."

"Oh, sorry to hear that. What's wrong with him?"

"My mam said he has the chicken pox."

"Ah, chicken pox isn't too bad. It's nothing to get so worked up about. My nephew had it once and he got on alright. Only stayed in bed for a few days."

"Oh. Well, I had better go now. I have some shopping to do" said Therese anxious to get away in case Mabel asked her any more questions to which she could not reply.

"Ta ra then," said Mabel.

Therese scuttled back to her room and looked in her purse to check how much money she had. To her horror there was not enough to buy the towels which she needed to take to the doctor's! Oh, mother of God, what will I do now? There was nothing for it but to call on

Irene and ask her if she could lend her some money. Thanks be to God I have the funds put away for the abortion.

She knocked on Irene's door but there was no answer.

Oh, where is she?

She knocked again and then just as she had given up hope, she heard the stairs creak and there was Irene encumbered with a string bag of groceries.

"Oh, Therese, are you looking for me?"

"Yes, I was."

"Well, come in dear," said Irene putting the key in the lock.

"I have been wondering how you were."

Therese followed Irene who put her bag of groceries on the table. She told Therese to take a seat which she did and, before her courage deserted her, she asked Irene if she could borrow some money until she was paid at the cafe.

"Of course, I will lend you the money, Therese. But I hope it is for something worthwhile" Irene said as she had noticed the traces of despair in her red puffy eyes.

"Oh, yes, it is."

"Well, I'm pleased to hear it."

She took her bag and withdrew her purse from which she took 2 shillings.

"Will that be enough dear?" asked Irene as she gave the money to Therese.

"Oh, yes thank you, it will be more than enough, and I will return it to you as soon as I get paid."

"There's no hurry dear. Now, would you like a cup of tea? I know I would."

"Oh, well, if it's not too much trouble." replied Therese as she looked at the coins in her hand, visualising handing them over to the chemist. God, it will be so embarrassing having to buy all those towels. I hope there won't be any customers in the shop.

"There, kettle's on." said Irene settling herself down in the chair.

"Now, how have you been lately? We haven't had a good chat for a while."

Therese looked down and rubbed the shilling.

Then her eyes welled with tears again and through them she blurted out to Irene the sorry tale of her life. She even told her of her appointment with the doctor tomorrow night and begged Irene to accompany her and afterwards, take her back here to her room.

"Oh, Therese, dear" Irene soothed putting her arms around her trembling shoulders.

"Do you really think that is what you should be doing?" she asked worriedly "I mean, there have been reports of girls having died in such places!"

"Oh, I can't let myself think about that!" she cried.

"It's just that I can't keep this baby. I can't. I'm here on my own and there is no one who will help me. Who is going to mind it while I work?" she sobbed.

"But, dear" interjected Irene, "Why don't you go to one of those places who adopt the babies out?"

"I've thought about that, but I couldn't bear to give it up to strangers after I've carried it in my belly for nine months. No, I've made the decision and I'm going tomorrow night!"

"Well, dear, if that's what you are going to do, then I cannot stop you. I will come with you and wait there to make sure you are alright. I would be beside myself with worry if you went on your own. You need your mother with you at times like this."

Therese sniffed and rubbed at her eyes.

"My mother thinks I am already away in the convent for unmarried mothers. I will go to hell for sure for all the lies I have told her in my letters."

Irene got up and poured the tea. She put a good measure of sugar in Therese's cup as she knew the girl was in a highly emotional state.

"Here" she said handing Therese the tea.

"Drink this. A good, sweet cup of tea is just what you need right now."

Therese took the cup and sipped at the hot tea feeling only slightly calmer.

"Thanks Irene, and thanks for giving me the money. Sorry I have been such a nuisance."

Irene reached over and patted Therese's hand.

"That's alright dear, but I really wish you would change your mind, I really do!"

Therese took another sip of tea, and undeterred stood up and thanked Irene again for her kindness. Irene told her she would be at her door tomorrow at 7.00pm giving them ample time to walk to the surgery.

After Therese had left, Irene sat down and pondered the terrible situation into which her young neighbour had been thrown. She wished with all her heart she would not go through with the abortion. Her mind thought about the cases of which she had heard.

Poor desperate pregnant girls, bleeding to death in the hands of backyard abortionists. It was too terrible to contemplate. I will just have to pray to God that Therese will be one of the fortunates who will come through the ordeal unscathed. Although her mind won't be, she will probably carry the guilt of destroying her child for the rest of her life.

Wednesday dawned cold and overcast as Irene awoke. She lay in her bed, her mind awhirl with what would eventuate on this day. Judy was scheduled to have the shock treatment at 11.00am. Professor Mumford had advised of this in a letter, at the bottom of which Irene had to sign giving her permission on behalf of her sister. This Irene had done with a good deal of angst and also hope, that Judy would benefit from this treatment, to be restored to some kind of normality, and be able to leave that terrible mad house at Helingly.

As she got up, her gaze drifted to the window. Scribbled over with frost, she discerned through it only grey. How appropriate, Irene thought that there was no blue sky or brilliant sunshine to lift the spirits. She thought of poor Therese in her room down the hall and of what she was to put herself through tonight. Oh God, please help her and Judy survive their ordeals, she prayed as she put the kettle and an egg on to boil.

She ate her breakfast with no enjoyment, then, putting herself and her room to rights, set off on her journey to the asylum where her sister's life would either be improved or totally destroyed.

It was 10.45 when Irene arrived at Helingly. She hurried straight to Judy's room to find it empty. Oh heavens, she thought, don't tell me I got the time wrong, and Judy has had the treatment already. She located one of the nurses who was familiar and asked her where her sister was.

"Oh, she would be in the pre-treatment room, waiting her turn I imagine." The nurse explained hastening to the isolation ward from which screams were emerging.

"But where is that?" Irene called after her, but she was not in ear shot leaving Irene in a panic desperate to locate her sister before she underwent the treatment. She had to be with her. She could not let her be there by herself. She looked around but there was no body to ask. But just as she was giving up all hope of finding someone, an orderly hove into view. She immediately pounced on him.

"Oh, excuse me, but could you tell me where the pre-treatment room is?" she gabbled.

"I can, and you can come with me as that is where I am headed." He told her.

"Thank you" Irene responded effusively as she tried to keep up with his loping strides.

"You see, I was told my sister is in this room and I need to be with her before she has this shock treatment." She explained.

They continued on along the corridor, turned right and then descended in a lift two floors down. They came to a door on which was written PRE-TREATMENT ROOM. NO ADMITTANCE. Seeing this, Irene's face fell.

"Oh, can't I go in there now?" she asked the orderly.

"Ah, take no notice of that" he reassured her.

He opened the door and let Irene through and there before her were four gurneys containing patients one of which was Judy.

Irene tip-toed over to her sister who she could now see was strapped to the gurney, her eyes filled with terror.

"Judy, I'm here. Don't be scared dear. There's nothing to be afraid of." She soothed knowing that Judy would probably not be calmed.

The orderly had disappeared into the next room which was the actual treatment room and immediately returned with an inmate on another gurney who had just undergone his therapy and was about to be taken back to the ward. Irene noticed that although somewhat dazed, he looked normal enough, so she was more or less reassured Judy would survive the ordeal.

No sooner had they departed when the treatment room door opened, and another orderly appeared ready to wheel in the next patient which happened to be Judy.

"Oh, can I go with her?" asked Irene anxiously as the orderly commenced wheeling the gurney.

"Well," said the orderly "You can if you feel you can cope with the procedure. Some people find it rather upsetting."

Irene replied.

"I will be alright. I would rather be with her than waiting here not knowing what's going on."

The trio entered the room and Judy was wheeled into a curtained section behind which stood a huge machine from which an assortment of wires protruded.

A nurse who was standing by the machine asked Irene.

"Are you a relative?"

"Yes, I am her sister."

"Very well, you may stay seeing you are family. It is hospital policy not to admit anyone who isn't family. Just stand at the end of the gurney and we ask that you be silent during the procedure."

Irene did as she was bid and stood quietly although her calmness was betrayed by the twisting of the handles of her bag.

The nurse wrapped a band around Judy's forehead above her terror stricken eyes and jammed a rubber object into her mouth. Ensuring she was securely strapped in, she then flicked a switch on the machine.

Now electrically charged, Judy's body went into spasm and started jerking violently. Irene's hand flew to her mouth in horror and, it was after a few minutes that she realised the scream she had heard in the room was hers.

Chapter Six

"Can I help you?"

Therese was in the pharmacy about to purchase the sanitary towels which she needed for tonight's appointment and she was not the only customer in the shop. There were two other people standing at the counter and they were men.

Face red with embarrassment, she whispered.

"Could I have four packets of Kotex please?"

"Pardon, what was it you wanted?" asked the pharmacist who was an elderly gentleman obviously hard of hearing.

Now, squirming with shame, feeling like some sort of criminal, she repeated.

"Four packets of Kotex please."

At that moment she wanted the floor to open up and take her down into the depths never to be seen again.

"Oh, very good" replied the pharmacist.

"I'll see what we have in stock."

He wandered off into the back room leaving Therese standing there with the male customers whose eyes she could feel burning into her soul. Her heart was racing. She felt like she had come in to hold up the shop! God, please let him hurry up so I can be out of here.

At last, he appeared with her supplies and then took his time wrapping them up in brown paper.

"There you are" he said handing Therese the parcel.

"That will be one shilling thank you."

Therese fumbled in her purse and as she withdrew the money it dropped to the floor.

One of the men retrieved it and gave it to her. Face, now on fire, she gave the money to the pharmacist and scuttled out the door clutching her parcel.

Mother of God that was terrible to be sure, she thought as she made her way along the street. I would have to be served by someone who was half deaf, and there would have to be men in the shop. I thought I would die from the shame there and then, and I still have to get through tonight! Oh, please God, help me through this!

She hurried on to the post office where her mam's expected letter was awaiting her collection. She put it into her bag, then stopped to buy two cans of soup which would hopefully tide her over until she was paid on Friday. Oh God, please let me be alright by Friday and not be in some class of hospital, she thought as she walked home. I must not think about such things. Think positive, Therese, just like mam does. Always look on the bright side she used to say back home in Dublin, when everything was getting her down and her Da was out on the drink.

She arrived home and, after putting the soup on to heat, settled down on the bed and opened her mam's letter.

Dublin
15th April 1950
Dear Therese,

It was grand to get your letter and to hear you are going alright at the convent and making some friends there. Everyone hereabouts still think you are away in London and getting lots of experience in the hospitality. That nosey parker Iris up the way in Albert Street keeps asking the questions about when you will be back and what happened to the feller you had. I told her you would rather have a good job away in London than go gallivanting around with him the docker that he was. That seemed to shut her up. She was always the one for poking the nose in.

Nessie is doing well with the reading. Sure she will be top of the class but Donal is still lazy. I have the devil of a time getting him out of the bed in the morning. He doesn't like school said he has been picked on again by that bruiser Mickey O'Leary. I will have to tell the teacher or his mother so I will. He should be taught a lesson.

Your Da has been off work. His chest has been playing up again. The doctor said it's the bronchitis. I hope he gets better soon as he doesn't get paid when he is sick but at least he isn't down the pub drinking away the money like he usually does.

You remember Bernadette Boyle who married Dylan O'Connell? Well, now the marriage is on the rocks. He was having a bit on the side with the hussy who works behind the bar at The Crown. One of Bernadettes' friends caught him canoodling with her while Bernadette was in the hospital having the twins! I always thought he looked a bit sly that Dylan. Now Bernadette is going to move back in with her parents and them with no room to swing a cat. Lord only knows how they are all going to fit in there.

Poor old Mother Branigan passed away last week. God rest her soul. It was a blessing in the end, she had been in bad health. Had the stomach trouble for as long as I can remember. I used to tell her to see the doctor, but she used to say it was only the digestive trouble and nothing to be worried about. She was tough as old nails, to be sure. Brought up fourteen kids in that little house in Tipperary with no help from that brute of a husband knocking her around and drinking away the money.

There was a requiem mass at Our Lady Help of Christians then some good craic at the pub on the corner. All the neighbours came and ten of her children were there with their children. Talking of children Therese. Now be strong and don't be worried about having the baby. Sure, didn't I have you and Nessie and Donal with no trouble at all? I'm sure the nuns will look after you and make sure they find a good home for the little one and you can come home again with your head high.

Well, that is all the news
Take care of yourself and God bless.
Your loving Mother

Therese put down the letter and, with a sigh, went over to pour the soup into the bowl. As she sat down to drink it, her eyes alighted on the parcel of sanitary napkins she had bought and her mind was filled with the guilt of deceiving her Mother. With every spoonful of soup she sent up a prayer to Mary and any other saints who might be listening, to help her survive and be forgiven for the terrible sin she was later to commit in Argyll Street.

The afternoon went by as Therese's anxiety increased and, as the hands of Therese's clock crept towards 7.15, the ominous knock of her neighbour sounded at the door.

With shaking hands, she slowly opened it and admitted Irene who wordlessly gave Therese a hug.

"Are you alright dear?" asked Irene registering the paleness of Therese's face.

"Yes, just a bit jittery, that's all."

"Oh, Therese, I wish you would not go through with this. I really do."

Therese mustered up whatever courage was left and answered.

"No, I cannot back out now. I've made up my mind and I'm going through with it. Now we'd better get going. The doctor said I had to be there at 7.30 sharp and it's nearly that now!"

She picked up the brown paper parcel and placed it into her bag then she and her neighbour set off down the stairs, out of the building, and into the fog shrouded night.

They walked along in silence. Irene's mind was awash with the condition of her sister and the fate which awaited Therese. Therese tried to extinguish any thoughts relating to the ordeal ahead and instead concentrated on putting one foot in front of the other until eventually they arrived at the surgery.

"I will wait for you here." Irene said sitting down on one of the chairs in the waiting area as Therese was escorted by a slovenly looking woman into a room along the hall.

She noticed that the carpet appeared to be grubby and the only reading matter was old, dog-eared magazines full of half-naked busty women. So, Irene sat clenching her hands and tried to imagine she was somewhere other than the place she was now, and she was transported back to the asylum.

After Irene had witnessed her sister's ordeal at the hands of the psychiatric nurse, she had been escorted out of the treatment room to recover from the shock. She had been admonished by the nurse who had said she should not have entered in the first place if she knew she would not be able to endure it.

Irene's despair had plunged into deeper depths as she had sipped the sweetened tea which a kind orderly had given her with words of sympathy, as the gurney containing Judy was wheeled past her back to the ward.

"But will she be alright?" asked Irene.

The orderly patted her hand.

"She'll be right after a good sleep. The treatment sometimes makes them sleep for 24 hours. Now, you just stay here and finish the rest of your tea and I'll return in a few minutes to take you back to the foyer."

"Oh, thank you, but I think I remember where to go."

Finishing her tea, Irene had made her way to the lift hoping she would not encounter anyone with whom she had to converse, her mind being filled with the images of poor Judy's body writhing from the shock.

Fortunately, she was the only passenger in the lift which spat her back into the corridor, right into the pandemonium of what was known as a Code Red alert. Orderlies and nurses were chasing an inmate who had escaped from the secure section of the isolation ward. Armed with a hypodermic needle which he had managed to grab from a nurse he was now coming towards Irene screaming and threatening to kill everyone in the building.

"Run, run for your life." An orderly yelled at Irene.

Irene started to run her heart beating so fast she thought it would burst from her chest, as she visualised the demented creature plunging the needle into her back and she dying from it or from the shock.

I can't die here in this place. I can't. I won't. Who will be there for Judy? She tried to run faster but as she thought she could not run any more, she suddenly heard a bang and voices shouting that they had finally captured the escapee. She stopped running and turning around saw the inmate being wrestled to the floor by six burly orderlies who had relieved him of his weapon and were now placing him into a straitjacket.

Meanwhile, Therese was now lying upon the examination couch trembling with fear, waiting for the doctor to appear to relieve her of this terrible burden. She tried focussing on the stain on the ceiling, the one which had reminded her the last time of the map of Tasmania, but tonight her mind stayed firmly in this room.

The door opened and Therese sat up. The doctor appeared wearing a white coat bespattered with bright red blood making her recoil in horror.

"Now" said the doctor pushing her back onto the couch "Let's get this over with, shall we? I'm running late as it is. Bend your knees and open your legs, and for Christ's sake keep still. That other one didn't do as I said and she paid for it!"

"Aren't I going to have an anaesthetic?" she croaked panic stricken.

"Anaesthetic for this?" he expostulated.

He brandished a steel instrument which Therese could see was already stained with someone else's blood and paralysed with fear could not will her legs to move.

"I said, open your legs, you stupid bitch" he snarled, roughly prising her legs open.

Suddenly, Therese came to her senses. She pushed his hand away sending the instrument clattering to the floor, then threw herself off the couch.

"I can't do this! I can't!" she screamed. Landing on the floor she knocked over a bowl which, to her sheer horror, contained the remnants of a bloody foetus.

"Aah!"

Stumbling from the room, she fell into the arms of her neighbour who had heard the commotion and was about to find out what was happening.

"Oh, Irene" she sobbed "please, please, get me out of here now!"

Chapter Seven

After Therese's traumatic time at the doctor's on Wednesday, Irene had escorted her back to the lodging house and put her to bed with a hot water bottle and a cup of warm milk laced with a shot of medicinal brandy which she had obtained from Arthur. She had stayed until sleep claimed her which took some time as, between sobs, Therese had felt the need to regale her neighbour with all the graphic details of her time in the room of horrors.

Irene knew the poor girl had to offload onto someone, so she did not attempt to stop her. She felt so sorry she found herself offering to help mind the baby when it arrived, which compounded her concerns about Judy living with her if she improved.

Professor Mumford had telephoned and told her that Judy had slept for nearly 24 hours and, although she appeared calmer, she still stayed mute. He had said that it was a matter of time in cases such as hers and not to lose hope for a recovery.

I will just have to cross that bridge when I come to it, she thought. I can't abandon this poor Therese after what she has just been through.

When she saw that she was asleep, she quietly washed the cup and turning the light out crept along to her room. Thoroughly exhausted from the day's events, she was overtaken by sleep from which she did not awaken until 9.00am the next morning.

"Hello" Irene called knocking on Therese's door "Are you awake Therese?"

After a few minutes the door opened to reveal a bedraggled Therese with hair awry.

"Oh, Irene, come in. I must look terrible to be sure!"

Irene came in and put her arm around her young neighbour.

"Now, don't you be worried how you look as long as you feel alright. Did you sleep?"

"Oh yes, I did. I slept like a log; thanks be to God. I thought I would be lying awake all the night thinking about my problems."

"Well, I'm glad you slept. The brandy and milk must have worked."

"Oh, did you give me some?" asked Therese now sitting on her bed.

"Yes, I got some brandy from Arthur and put it into the milk I warmed up. You certainly needed it, the state you were in."

"Thank you for looking after me." Said Therese eyes cast down.

"That's the least I could do."

"Now" added Irene patting Therese's hand "What are your plans? Are you going to work tomorrow at that cafe you were telling me about?"

Therese looked at her neighbour.

"Yes, I am. I must earn some money now I'm having the baby." She replied her hands moving protectively over her stomach.

"And don't forget, Therese, what I said last night about helping you out with the little one."

"No, Irene. I can't thank you enough for that." replied Therese eyes now glistening with tears.

"To be sure, I don't know where I'd be without your support, I really don't."

"Well," Irene said brightly "You must try to eat something now. What do you feel like? Would you like me to make you an egg or some toast? Now you are going ahead with the pregnancy, you must take care of yourself."

"Oh, I don't really feel like much in the morning as I usually don't feel well."

"Maybe I will have a piece of dry toast. Sometimes that works."

"Very good. Then I will make that for you."

Irene went over and put a slice of bread under the grill.

"What about a cup of tea? I know I could do with another one."

"Oh, alright, thanks Irene."

While the toast was grilling and the kettle boiling, Therese put on the clothes she had been wearing yesterday.

"I think you might need a couple of maternity outfits, Therese. That skirt doesn't look like it will fit you for much longer" said Irene as she poured the tea and noticed the undone button on the skirt.

"Oh, I know. Everything is getting too tight, but I can't afford to buy anything at the moment and the money I was going to give that doctor last night, well I've put that away for the baby's expenses."

She came over and sat at the table.

"Yes, that was wise," Irene replied bringing over the toast and tea.

She placed it on the table and sat down.

"You know," she said, "There's a secondhand shop down the road which used to sell a few maternity outfits. How about we make our way there this morning and have a look. I will buy you something, my treat!"

"Oh, Irene, I can't let you do that!" exclaimed Therese as she bit off a piece of the toast.

"Fiddlesticks" replied Irene "I don't need to buy any clothes and you do so there's an end to it!"

"Well, only if you're sure. I don't want to be like a charity case. When I get paid, I will pay you back only it might take some time. I won't be getting much."

Irene sipped her tea.

"Now don't you be worrying yourself about it."

Therese then thought about the parcel of sanitary towels which she would no longer need. She could ask for her money back. However, the thought of returning them to the chemist and the ensuing humiliation soon banished that thought from her mind.

It must have been telepathy, as at that moment, Irene piped up.

"You could take those towels back to the chemist and ask for a refund. I'm sure Mr Abernathy would be agreeable."

Seeing the look of horror on Therese's face Irene knew it would be embarrassing for her to do that, so she offered to do the deed for her.

"Oh, would you? I was so embarrassed having to buy them in the first place. You wouldn't believe! There were two men in there. I thought I would die of the shame and then I had to drop the change on the floor to make matters worse!"

That made them both laugh.

"Well, if they are in there when I turn up with the parcel, they will all wonder what is going on, and that's for sure!" Irene joked knocking over the tea in the process.

That made them laugh even more and it was some time after they had cleaned up that the two neighbours eventually left the building. The older one carried a string bag containing a brown paper parcel while the younger one now with a less heavy heart, trotted along beside her.

They arrived at the second- hand shop after Irene had returned the parcel to the chemist. Therese had waited outside happy that she did not have to confront Mr Abernathy again and, when Irene had emerged minus the parcel and bearing the shilling in her hand, she was happier still.

After they had looked at the three maternity outfits which was all that was available in the shop, Therese eventually decided on a pair of black pants and a blue smock top with a bow on the front, Irene saying she would look one of the best dressed mothers-to-be in the neighbourhood.

Handing over the money she then exclaimed that all the shopping had made her hungry and suggested that they repair to a cafe for some tea and a sandwich.

Therese also suddenly felt like something to eat as all she had had was the piece of toast which Irene had given her that morning.

"This looks like a good place" announced Irene as they came across a cafe not far from the second-hand shop.

"Let's go in here."

They found a table near the window and Therese sat down gratefully now aware of the tiredness in her legs. She thought of tomorrow and the days after that when she would be on her feet serving in the cafe and wondered how she was going to cope.

"What would you like to eat dear?" asked Irene as she perused the menu.

"Oh, just a cheese sandwich, thank you Irene."

"And tea? Would you like some? Or maybe you should have a glass of milk." Suggested Irene looking at Therese's stomach.

"Yes, I suppose milk would be better."

The waitress came over and took their order. A cheese sandwich and milk for Therese and a spam with pickle and tea for Irene.

"Irene" said Therese.

"Yes, dear."

"I really appreciate what you are doing for me and I hope one day I can help you out in some way."

"Oh, that's alright Therese. We must all try to help each other when we can. I have been helped by people in the past. What goes around, comes around is what I always say."

Therese said.

"With all my troubles, I forgot to ask you about your sister. How is she going?"

Irene told her Judy had undergone shock treatment and the prognosis of the Professor sounded hopeful. She did not tell her of the barbarism of the treatment nor of the terrible things she had witnessed at the asylum. Her young friend had been through enough trauma lately without Irene adding any more.

"Here we are then" chirped the waitress.

"Cheese and milk, spam and tea."

"Thank you" they both chorused.

As Therese bit into her sandwich, she said to Irene.

"Would you mind if I came to visit your sister the next time you go? Only it will have to be on Sundays as Saturdays will be taken up with the chores and I will be working the other days."

"No, I wouldn't mind dear, but I must warn you, you might see and hear some things which might shock you. The asylum is not a very cheerful place. And Judy does not speak."

"I'll take my chances" said Therese taking a sip of the milk which left a white mark on her top lip.

Irene reached across and smiling, wiped it off with the serviette.

Therese smiled back and they finished their meal in companionable silence.

Chapter Eight

Therese had been waitressing at the cafe now for the last two months and was feeling more fatigued as the days went by. Her shifts were from Monday to Friday 10.00am until 4.00pm.while the weekend was taken up with household chores and shopping for food. She had managed to see a doctor which Irene had recommended and who had advised her to attend an antenatal clinic where she would be told about breathing techniques for the birth. This she had dismissed as nonsense. Her ma had not gone in for any of that palaver and she had delivered her babies without trouble. No, Therese did not have time for that, there was enough going on in her life as it was.

One afternoon she was coming home from her shift when she saw Irene going through the gate. She was carrying a suitcase and escorting a lady in a headscarf who she took to be her sister, Judy as her slow pace signified, she was rather unwell. Therese followed them in the door.

"Hello Irene" said Therese.

Irene turned around.

"Oh, Therese. I didn't realise you were right behind us. Judy has come to stay with me for the weekend."

"That's grand, to be sure," replied Therese.

"Yes, it is. Why don't you come in a bit later after I have her settled and we can have a cup of tea?"

"Oh, alright, thanks I will. I could do with a cup of tea and a sit down. My legs are aching terribly today. The cafe was so busy. There was a boatload of tourists and I was run off my feet!"

"You poor thing" replied Irene.

Slowly, Irene helped her sister up the creaking stairs with Therese following closely behind. Irene opened her door and manoeuvred Judy in.

"See you a bit later then, Therese" she said.

"Yes, ta ra."

Opening her door, Therese collapsed on the bed and thought she could go to sleep forever. She felt so tired but, as she lay there, she was aware of the baby's movements and her hands went immediately to rest on her stomach. God, she prayed, please let my baby be healthy and stay healthy and not be like one of those poor people in that asylum where Judy is. Mother of God, it was terrible to see those mad ones that day I went with Irene!

That one who was screeching about the world ending, running amok in the rec room pulling off her clothes and exposing herself, and those fierce looking guards around the place would give you the creeps for sure! I thought I would be alright, but I should have taken Irene's advice and stayed away. Now Judy is here for the weekend. God, I hope she won't have any turns! I will have to make sure the door is locked! But surely, they wouldn't have let her out of there if they thought she was a threat to anyone's safety.

She closed her eyes and before long was awoken by a knock on the door.

"Therese" she heard a voice call out.

"Are you ok?"

Therese realised it was Irene.

She went to the door.

"Oh, sorry Irene, I must have dozed off."

"That's alright, dear. I thought you might have gone to sleep. I made the tea and there is some cake if you would like some."

"Yes, thanks I would. I'll just tidy my hair and I'll be right with you."

"Don't bother with that, dear. It's just Judy and me. Just come as you are."

So, Therese shut her door and went with her neighbour.

As they entered, Judy's face registered a modicum of expression which was a great improvement to the vacant look which she usually exhibited, making Therese feel slightly less discomfited.

Therese noticed a camp bed resting in the corner which she presumed must have been purloined from Mabel as the bed in which Irene slept would not have accommodated two people. She probably charged Irene a rental fee for that at weekend rates into the bargain!

Irene told Therese to sit on the armchair which was more comfortable for someone in her condition. Judy was sitting on the kitchen chair which Irene thought she would prefer as it was similar to the one on which she sat in the asylum, and Irene's perch was her bed.

Irene poured the tea. She handed Therese a cup and a plate on which sat a slice of sponge cake, then she went over to her sister and asked her if she wanted some too. Judy nodded at Irene who poured her some tea, Therese noticing her putting in liberal amounts of sugar. Irene brought over the tea and cake to Judy and, bending down, broke off a piece which she gave to Judy. Without delay, Judy stuffed it into her mouth and then indicated she wanted some more.

"Now, Judy" admonished Irene.

"Don't eat so quickly. I don't want you choking on me over the weekend!"

She gave her the cup the handle of which Judy shakily curled her fingers around and Irene monitored the progress of tea to mouth. There was only a minute amount spilled as the saucer testified to the relief of Irene.

"There, good girl." She praised as she took the cup and saucer and placed it on the table.

"Hardly a drop spilled."

"Judy looks better than the last time I saw her" announced Therese as she tried to settle more comfortably in the chair, the baby now making its presence felt.

"Yes, I think so too" replied Irene as she looked over at her sister whose eyes were now assessing her surroundings.

"Did Mabel lend you the camp bed, or did she rent it to you?" asked Therese.

"She wanted a shilling for it. Said she could have asked for more but seeing as I was a long-term resident thought she was doing me a favour."

"That would be typical of the old skin flint," replied Therese biting into the remainder of the cake.

"Always charging like a wounded bull. And she gets away with it! You should have told her you wouldn't pay."

"I know, Therese, but I had to have the bed. I didn't have any choice. I didn't know anyone who would lend me one for the weekend."

"No, I suppose you didn't. But if Judy improves and she leaves the asylum, will she come here to live with you? It's going to be pretty cramped in here!"

Irene went over and gave Judy more tea.

"Yes, dear, I have thought about that eventuality. I was going to ask Mabel for that double room on the top floor. The one that married couple had. From what I remember it had lots of light. Better than here, which gets a bit dark when there is no sun."

"Oh, that would be better for you both, although you will have extra stairs to climb!"

"Yes, I had thought of that too, but we will just have to manage one way or the other."

"Now" she added.

"Have you been to those breathing classes yet dear, the ones the doctor told you about?"

"No, I haven't. Don't seem to have time or the energy what with working at the cafe all week. I'm just about done in by the weekend!"

"Why don't you take a sick day and get yourself to a class? Even if you only go to one, at least you will be told how to do the breathing. I'm sure it will help you at the birth, dear."

Therese contemplated what her neighbour had said and replied that she would think about it but inwardly thought, breathing classes! What is there to learn about breathing for goodness sake, sure it is all natural?

"Have you seen Mr Curtis lately?" asked Therese now anxious to change the subject of breathing.

"No, I haven't. I was going to look in on him but what with one thing and another I didn't get around to it. When Judy goes back on Sunday, I will pop in. The last time I saw him he was telling me about his grandson. Apparently, he is doing well in the hospitality. He's the bar and lounge manager at the hotel in Bournemouth."

"I had better contact him and ask for some details of life in a hotel as that is where mam's neighbours all think I am," Therese replied.

"In some classy place away in London, working my way up the career ladder. But little do they know where I really am, and what I look like. Like a beached whale and no mistake! That would set their tongues wagging!"

Irene looked at Therese and it was to the sound of giggling, that the expression on Judy's face was one which had not appeared since the days before her admission to the asylum.

Chapter Nine

"Sorry I haven't been in to see you lately, Arthur."

It was Monday and Irene had popped in to see her elderly neighbour. The weekend had ended with Judy being escorted by her sister back to the asylum at 4.00pm on Sunday. Apart from Judy tossing and turning in Irene's bed (Irene having taken the camp bed) and a short episode of pulling her hair, the weekend had gone as well as could have been expected. On Saturday, Irene had taken Judy for a trip on the bus to the pier where they had partaken of a sandwich and tea at Therese's cafe. Irene had introduced herself and Judy to Dot the manageress as Therese had instructed her to, after she had heard they might be going there. She had been invited to come with them but, because she was occupied with the chores and felt so tired, she had declined. Also, it was the last place she would have wanted to be after working there all the week!

After their lunch which Judy seemed to have enjoyed, devouring her sandwich in record time, they had walked along the pier. The cawing of the seagulls diving and swooping over the water had Judy intrigued, and they had spent an inordinate amount of time looking at them. Irene was glad she had brought their cardigans as they were buffeted by a strong breeze as they walked along towards the end of the pier.

There were a few fishermen casting their lines into the water and it was there also that Judy had stopped, seemingly oblivious to the wind whipping her hair into her eyes, and the saltwater spraying her clothes. She certainly seems to enjoy being here by the seaside, thought Irene as she glimpsed what was a tenuous smile cross her sister's face, as a wave dashed itself against one of the pylons. I wonder if it has brought back any memories when she was with that boyfriend of hers. Maybe he had taken her to the seaside, and she had retained some sort of happy recollection of her time there. Irene then noticed there was a small kiosk a short distance away, so she had enticed Judy away from the fishermen with the promise of a vanilla ice cream. This had proved to be the highlight of Judy's day as with every lick of the confection she seemed to have been transported into a happier, more peaceable place.

"It's good to see you again, Irene." said Arthur as Irene sat in her usual spot.

"I have had Judy staying with me on the weekend."

"Oh, is that right? She must be improving if they let her go on weekend leave. The treatment must have worked then?"

"Yes, I really think it has made a difference, Arthur but, as the Professor advised, it could be only temporary and she might have a relapse, but for the moment she seems not too bad. I took her down to the pier on Saturday for a bite to eat and she was mesmerised by the whole place: the seagulls, the fishermen, she even didn't mind the wind or the saltwater spraying her clothes, and when she licked an ice cream her face was in raptures. I think Arthur, between you and me, she had been to the seaside with that boyfriend of hers and has retained some happy memories!"

Arthur leaned over.

"You could be right, my dear. It really does sound like she is getting better."

He added.

"And talking of boyfriends, I heard from Betty."

Arthur's daughter was now living in Lourmarin, a medieval village not far from Aix En Provence in the south of France. After a rather messy divorce from which she had emerged quite a deal wealthier, she had firstly helped Ben with the lease of a small bedsit, then she had gone to a travel agent and booked a month's holiday in Provence. There, among the aroma of the lavender, her bruised flesh and her ego were slowly healed. It was also where she had met Antoine, the one who brought her the happiness which she had not received in her previous relationship.

They had met by chance on market day when all the artisans came from the outlying villages to Provence in an attempt to sell their wares, Lourmarin being the village most represented as many artists were residing there.

Betty had stopped to admire an artist's work which was a painting of the village replete with the renaissance chateau atop the hill. Antoine was also admiring it and a conversation had been struck between him and the artist about how the essence of the village had been captured.

"Mon ami, c'est une belle peinture!" Antoine had exclaimed to the artist.

Then, directing a question at Betty he asked in English.

"Do you not think so Madam?"

"Oh, yes" replied Betty "I love it. Is this village nearby?" she asked.

"Oui, it is my village. You have not seen it?"

"No, I have only been here in Provence. I am here on a holiday."

"Ah, an English woman on holiday! Maybe I can buy her a cafe and croissant and tell her of the 'ow you say, the beautes of Lourmarin."

"Oh, you mean the beauties?"

"Tres bien, the beauties!"

So, in a tiny cafe nearly hidden under trailing vines, over cafe au lait and croissants au chocolat, Betty had succumbed to the charms of this Frenchman as he regaled her with the details of his life.

He was an author and had attained a scholarship to study literature at the Sorbonne in Paris where he had lived on the Left Bank with some fellow students, one of with whom he had fallen in love. However, his love had not been returned as she had bequeathed it to a poet whom she had met in a smoky bar in the 10th arrondisement, while Antoine had been studying.

This had upset him greatly which led to failures in his exams. After imbibing too many red wines and smoking too many Gauloises, he decided to leave the Sorbonne and take his broken heart back to the village where he was born. He had moved back in with his parents who were dismayed that he had left the University. They had been proud that their only son had done so well and been accepted at the Sorbonne, all the village apprised of his success.

However, after all the disappointment had dissolved and Antoine's tragedy had been supplanted by fresh gossip of others' misfortunes, Antoine had devoted his time to writing. His inspiration was garnered through the window of his tiny attic bedroom as his eyes beheld the beauty before him, and he wondered how he ever could have left this idyllic spot, to not hear the cawing of the eagles and kites, to not smell the aromas of the lavender, to not wake to the wondrous light in which the area was bathed.

All these things he had missed when he had lived in Paris where he had always felt homesick. Even when he was on top of the Eiffel Tower with the wonders of the city laid before him. When he was in the cloisters of Notre Dame and the bells were tolling for prayer, when he walked along the Seine and over the bridges he still felt apart from this city, like a cut flower left devoid of water, to wilt and die.

His first work was a short story about an eagle who had befriended a boy in a village high up in the alps. He had sent it to a publishing house on Rue Cambon. They had returned it with a covering letter stating that although it was well written, there was a limited market for such work and wished him well in his future endeavours.

Not to be deterred, he spent many hours up in his garret while his father downstairs lamented his son's lack of income. His father was a baker working in the boulangerie in the village as his father had before him, and his days commenced long before the sun rose. His mother took in washing and ironing for the wealthier residents, chief among them was the mayor, his wife and their three daughters who always looked impeccable strolling around the village in their finery, testament to Antoine's mother's labours.

Many arguments ensued at night when, over dinner, Antoine's father would rail at his son about the time he wasted up there in his room, with not a centime to show for it!

Mon dieu! What have I raised, why isn't he in the University where he should be, studying? When is he going to get a paying job? What about the olives which need picking or the grapes for the wine? On and on he went, while his mother manoeuvred the iron around the mayoral collars and tried to restore some peace. It would only be a matter of time she would say, when he would be successful and be paid accordingly, while secretly offering prayers to the saints, to please help her son be successful with his writing.

However, after one of many sleepless nights when he roused himself from his bed, and filled the basket with the discarded crumpled paper of his efforts, and the ashtray with his spent cigarettes, Antoine felt satisfied that he was ready to submit to the publisher the nearly completed manuscript he had been slaving over.

He had posted some chapters to the same firm who had rejected his previous work and prayed that this time he would finally attain the break he had been hoping for. His mother was the only person to whom he had told as he knew what would be the reaction of his father.

"Mon cher fils" "my dear son," exclaimed his mother embracing him in her strong arms and smelling of starch and clothes dried by the Provencal sun.

"I have been praying to the saints every day to send down success to you!"

"Merci, ma mere, but it is early days. The publisher might not like it. They did not like the other work I sent them."

He took a red apple from the dish and bit into it.

"Oui, I know Antoine, but that was only your first attempt, a little story, not an interesting novel like this one sounds!"

The novel he had written was more or less based on his own life growing up in a beautiful village in Provence, his hardworking parents making sacrifices for their son to obtain an education and go on to study in Paris, where he graduated with top honours. His meeting and falling in love with a girl who had stolen his heart, their betrothal in Notre Dame and then settlement in a tres elegant house in Provence, where he wrote another masterpiece up in his study as his three children gambolled in the garden below. He had written about the various characters living in the village, and of the mistral which blew for days, forcing the residents to take cover in their houses until it was calm enough to venture out.

The publisher had taken two months to contact Antoine who had presented himself at the post office every day in the hope of receiving the letter from Paris which would turn his life around. He always remembered that it was Friday, the 21st April when he received the letter. The day when the mistral was blowing its hardest, bending the trees and clearing the streets of souls who all had retreated behind closed doors. Antoine had found it nearly impossible to walk in such conditions but, finally he reached the post office, where he was handed the awaited envelope.

Resisting the urge to open it there and then, he buried it deep into the inside of his jacket and with his hood up, battled his way back home through the fierce wind which was now blowing flakes of snow into his eyes.

"Bonnes nouvelles?" Good news?" queried his mother peeping out from under a mound of ironing. She had noticed an excited look on Antoine's face as he bounded up the stairs to his room snowflakes falling from his jacket as he went.

He called over his shoulder.

"Oh, I hope so maman."

It was soon after, over glasses of pastis, the kitchen was filled with happiness, as mother and son hugged and cried over the letter which stated that the publishers had liked what he had written and had offered him an advance towards the completion of his book.

Now the rest was history, as Antoine had gone on to write many books. He had eventually married his literary agent and bought a beautiful house not far from his family home. As his parents were getting on in years, he wanted to be near if they needed help at any time. This of course was rejected by his father who wanted to remain independent as long as possible. He told his son to look after his own family as now they had a daughter who was the apple of her grandparents' eyes.

However, after a few years of marital bliss, one of the mountains of the Alpes de Haute was responsible for taking the life of Antoine's wife, as she skied down a slope straight into a tree and was killed instantly. It took some time for Antoine to recover from the loss, and he sold the marital home which held too many memories for him to bear.

After the removal van had left, he and his daughter had followed in the Renault packed with his books and all the miscellaneous items collected over the time of his marriage and had driven straight to his old family home to live with and care for his parents.

He had been there only for a year when, in the middle of his sixth novel, his father developed, "baker's disease", a lung condition due to the wheat flour which he had inhaled over the many years working in the boulangerie.

This had proved to be fatal, and Aimee lost her pappa two days short of her third birthday. Her grand-mere, never recovering from the loss of her beloved husband, followed him into the grave not long after.

So Antoine continued to live alone with Aimee in the family home until that day Betty caught his eye in the market place.

"I'm so pleased that she has found happiness at last." Irene said to Arthur as he finished relaying all the news contained in his daughter's letter.

"She certainly deserves it after what she has been through. And isn't it nice she gets on with her stepdaughter?" She's a sweet girl isn't she?" commented Irene as she looked at the photo which Arthur passed over to her.

"Yes, she looks a peach! I think she must be about twelve now. You know, Irene, Betty keeps on about me coming over there for a holiday and meeting them all."

"Well then, you should go. No time like the present they always say. What's to stop you? Might do you good to get out of this place for a while. Have a change of scenery. Do you the world of good, Arthur!"

Arthur rubbed his knee.

"Oh no, I'm too old for all that gadding about in foreign lands and the knee doesn't help much."

"Oh fiddlesticks! I'm sure you would be alright. Just go for a week. The knee will be the same wherever you are. You could catch the ferry over the channel, and I'm sure Betty would pick you up and drive you to their place."

"Yes, she said she would do that, but Irene, it all sounds too much to think about. Packing and so on."

"Go on with you, Arthur. What is there to pack but a change of underwear and a sweater or two? I can help you if you like."

"That's very good of you my dear. When I think of my time in the army when I had everything ship- shape. It wouldn't have taken me any time to pack my kit... but now!"

He exclaimed shaking his head and looking rather dispirited.

"Ah, where's the old fighting spirit eh? Onward and upward, I say!" Irene asseverated.

She stood up readying herself for departure.

"At least think about it Arthur."

Arthur stood supported by his stick.

"Yes, my dear, I will think about it and thank you for all your support."

"Nonsense" she said briskly "It's my pleasure. We all must look out for each other. See you again."

She kissed him on the cheek, noting the manly essence of tobacco and Brylcreem.

She walked out into the hall, past the sink, noticing the rust becoming more intense due to the constant dripping of the tap. She made her way down the creaking stairs just arriving before the hall light went out and then entered her room where she wished it was, she who had such an invitation to travel, as she would be off on the first ferry out of this place and no mistake!

Chapter Ten

Therese was anxiously awaiting the birth of her baby. On her feet at the cafe waiting on tables, she could not wait for her shift to end so she could go back to her room and put up her legs. The hospital into which the doctor had booked her was fortunately within walking distance and Irene had told her to let her know the minute there was any sign of the impending birth. The last time she had consulted the doctor he had told her that her blood pressure was rather high, and she was to rest as much as possible.

Irene had been a godsend as she had helped her with the washing and the shopping between visiting her sister at the asylum. Judy was to be discharged around the time of the baby's birth leaving Irene overjoyed at the news, and she had immediately asked Mabel if she could move into the bigger room on the top floor. Mabel had acceded to her request albeit demanding extra rent saying, "I could get a lot more for that room, you know, Irene but as you're a long term lodger, I'm only charging you an extra quid!" Irene did not have much choice as it was the only way that she could have Judy with her, and because she did not want to move to unfamiliar territory, she had agreed to the increase.

I don't know what I would have done without Irene, thought Therese as she lay on her bed this Sunday morning. She had not slept much during the night as the baby had been rather active preventing her from attaining a comfortable position. Also, she was now experiencing a lot of heartburn which added to her woes. She remembered her mother saying that the baby would have lots of hair if there was heartburn experienced towards the end of the pregnancy. Well, if that was the case, then this one would have the hair down to the waist to be sure! Her mother had been writing regular letters telling Therese of the usual gossip. How another old neighbour had left this mortal coil and how good the craic was at the wake. How too much Guiness had been consumed by one of the mourners leading to him being arrested by the Gardai for assaulting the publican and urinating on the street.

She wrote about one of the girls with whom Therese went to school, joining the convent to the jubilation of the family as good Catholics that they were, they had been sending novenas to our Lady to bestow the vocation on their seventh daughter.

She again told Therese not to be afraid of giving birth and giving the child up for adoption. When Therese read the letters she felt guilty about deceiving her mother but although it was going to be hard she knew in her heart she was doing the right thing keeping her child, and she her mother and family would be told in the fullness of time.

Therese slowly got up off the bed and lumbered over to the sink to boil the kettle for the tea when suddenly, she felt a wetness trickling down her legs and onto the floor. Then no sooner than that happened, she was overcome by a sharp pain in her back. God in heaven, it's coming! She made her way out of her room to alert Irene, feeling all the while the sticky wetness between her legs. Can't be worried about that, she thought as she knocked on her neighbour's door. There will be worse to come before the day is out!

"Therese!" exclaimed Irene when she noticed the state she was in.

"Is the baby coming dear?"

"Yes, I think it is. Oh, Irene, I wet myself and oh, I have another pain!" she cried grasping hold of her neighbour as the pain took hold.

"There, there, dear, don't worry. All's well."

Irene said reassuringly.

"Now, you just sit down here on the chair while I finish dressing and we will go straight off to the hospital."

Irene flew around dragging on some stockings and then putting on the clothes in which she had been yesterday.

Meanwhile, Therese had gone pale and was holding her stomach in an effort to quench another contraction which was about to engulf and swamp her with its ferocity.

Irene grabbed her bag and, helping Therese from the chair, she escorted her to her room where thankfully was a suitcase which Therese had packed a few weeks ago in readiness for the event. She also ensured Therese had the Woolworths "wedding ring" on her finger so the hospital would show her some respect.

The stairs seemed to creak more loudly as if in sympathy to Therese's plight, as Irene helped her down and out the front door to the hospital.

It was a slow journey, as every few minutes, Therese had to stop and lean on Irene as they waited for a contraction to pass. However, they eventually arrived, and Therese was immediately placed into a wheelchair to be rushed up to the labour ward, leaving Irene to bide her time in the room reserved for relatives and expectant fathers. These men, anxious for the news that their offspring had been safely delivered, were all pacing up and down, the smoke from their cigarettes seeping into every corner of the room making Irene feel like she was in the fug of the local hotel. Thinking of hotels, her mind drifted to the days when she was in such places, drinking herself into a stupor. Thank god I survived all that. I could have easily been on the front page of the Telegraph: 'Woman found dead in hotel room.' Thank god I went to the AA when I did. I must go to another meeting before Judy comes as I can't be taking her along there. I might meet Robert again. Such a nice tea we had- fish and chips. I enjoyed that.

Aroused from her musing, Irene was subsequently informed by a nurse that her daughter had just given birth to a boy weighing 8lbs 10ozs and both mother and baby were well. This news, as well as the idea that the nurse had taken her to be Therese's mother, left Irene consumed with relief and happiness and oblivious to the fug in which she was sitting.

Therese's quick labour had surprised her, as she had visions of having to endure interminable hours of agony. Now it was all over, and she was back in her room at Mabel's with Danny as she had named him, latched onto her breast suckling greedily.

Irene had brought Arthur to see her, and he had chucked Danny under the chin commenting what a bonny lad he was. Mabel had turned up with the queens, Mona and Rita, who were also enraptured, cooing over him and turning his tiny cheek red with their lipsticked kisses, as their overpowering perfume filled the air. They had chipped in and bought a teething ring and a bunch of daisies for which Therese was very thankful.

There were things Therese needed to buy for Danny, but as she had limited resources she would have to make do. For the moment, he was sleeping in the bottom drawer of the chest and she was bathing him in the sink. She knew this would suffice for the time being but would not be feasible when he grew bigger. She was going to cross that bridge when she came to it.

For now, she would just enjoy her baby as she put him onto her other breast and felt his tiny hand curl around her finger. As his blue eyes looked into hers, she knew she had done the right thing, and not aborted him or given him away to strangers. She noticed a bead of moisture on his red downy head to be joined by another and then realised it was her tears baptising him with maternal love. She had arranged to have him christened at the hospital by the priest who had wended his way into the ward on several occasions, to offer God's forgiveness to any of the mothers who felt in need of it. He had been only too willing to baptise little Danny bringing into the fold another of God's anointed. At least, Therese thought, as she watched the holy water trickle over his red head, mam won't be able to say that my Danny is nothing but a heathen, not baptised, and going to Limbo forever!

Over the following weeks, Therese found it was not easy caring for a new-born especially when there was colic involved. There was scarcely a night when Therese was not up pacing the floor with Danny in her arms as his cries filled the room with his pain and her with anguish. The worry of him disturbing the neighbours added to her woes as she envisaged Mabel throwing her and the baby out onto the street.

Danny seemed to sleep for Irene when she minded him during the day while Therese was at the cafe. It probably had to do with the outings on which he was taken as

Irene pushed him in the old perambulator with Judy tagging along. They would always go down to the pier where the fresh sea air seemed to settle him and also had the same calming effect on Judy. Therese would leave some expressed milk for Irene to feed him while Therese was at the cafe.

Arthur had found the perambulator in the street as he was walking home from his club. Knowing that Therese did not own one he had pounced on it and pushed it back with effort to Mabel's where he planned to tighten the wheels and give it a good clean. He was bemused by the passers-by as they peered into the carriage expecting to see a cherubic face staring back at them but to their disappointment they found nothing there.

"What the deuce are you doing with that contraption, Arthur?" asked Mabel coming from her room alerted to the noise of the carriage being manoeuvred through the front door.

"I found it on the street. It's for Therese," replied Arthur.

"It just needs a good clean and the wheels tightening, and it will be as good as new."

"Well, you can fix it up down here. You can't get it up them stairs. Hope it's not got any mice in it. Put it by the front door, when you've cleaned it up, in that corner."

She said pointing her finger to show Arthur where she meant.

"Right, you are then. Will do!" he exclaimed giving her a salute as though in the army.

So, Arthur had given it a good clean and after he had tightened and oiled the wheels, to the utter delight of Therese, he had presented it to her spic and span and she was quite overcome with the generosity of her old neighbour.

The sleepless nights were taking a toll on Therese and now added to her woes, her nipples were cracked and painful when Danny was nursing.

"Oh, Therese, don't get upset," soothed Irene as she witnessed her young neighbour's distress one afternoon as she tried to feed the baby.

"I can't take much more of it, Irene," she wailed.

"My nipples are so sore. It's agony when he feeds, and I'm so tired. Last night I was up and down with him. Mother of god, I wish this colic would go away!"

"Have you seen the doctor or been to the clinic? I think I remember when I was at the big house the cook saying that lanolin was used for sore nipples. Maybe I can go and buy you some from the pharmacy?"

"Oh" sniffed Therese trying to stuff the dummy into Danny's mouth in between his cries.

"Oh, Irene, I will try anything at the moment. There should be some change in my purse over there on the table."

Irene walked over and withdrew a shilling.

"I will go now dear before they close. Is there anything else you want while I'm at the shops? Have you got something for your tea?"

"Yes, thanks. I was going to heat some soup."

"Is that all you're having, dear? You must eat more than that to keep up your strength and your milk supply for the baby."

"I'll have some toast with the soup."

"Very well but do try to eat more. You should be having vegetables and some meat."

"Yes, I know, but that all takes time to prepare and cook and I don't seem to have the energy."

"Well, hopefully the babe will eventually get over the colic and give you a good night's rest."

"Oh, I do hope so, Irene. I feel so down at the moment."

"Now, think positive dear. This will pass."

"Now," she said briskly" I'll be off and be back in a jiffy with the lanolin."

Therese found the lanolin soothing and, following Irene's advice, went with Danny to see the nurse at the clinic where he was weighed. To Therese's horror, she was advised that her baby was not putting on weight due to the fact that her milk supply was down. She was advised to put the baby on the bottle which would satisfy her hungry baby and also give her nipples a chance to heal. Although Therese did not like the idea of relinquishing the breast feeds and the bonding which came from it, she knew in her heart that it was her only option. Her baby's crying could well have been due to hunger and not to the colic after all!

She put Danny into the perambulator and with a somewhat lighter heart pushed him to the pharmacy outside which she left him while she purchased another bottle and an extra teat. Then she bought two bottles of milk for Danny and called into the newsagents to buy the paper which she planned to read when she had a moment to spare. Pushing him home, she noticed he was asleep so she thought she would leave him where he was and not bother taking him out of the carriage and disturbing him. Let sleeping dogs lie, she thought. If I try and take him out, he will only wake up and I have too many things to do. I have to reply to mam's letter, the nappies have to be pegged out, and all his clothes. She had never imagined how many clothes a tiny baby could go through, and then her admiration for her mother would surface as now she knew how hard it was looking after a baby. At least her mother had her husband to support her, not like me, all alone. She thought how nice it would be to be married to someone she loved and who loved her and her precious Danny. Her thoughts took her to Mabel's and as she pushed the carriage through the door her landlady appeared, duster in hand.

"Been taking the lad for a walk have you?" she asked.

"Oh, hello Mabel, yes, I had to go to the clinic. Irene told me to. The nurse there told me I had to put Danny on the bottle because I haven't got enough milk for him. That what was why he had been crying. I thought it was the colic that was upsetting him."

"Oh, is that right? Well, needs must. Plenty of kiddies on the bottle and it don't do them no harm, so don't fret about that."

She saw Therese leaving Danny in the perambulator.

"Are you going to leave him there?"

"Yes, will that be alright? He will only wake up if I take him out, and I've got so many things to do. I can hear him if he starts crying."

"Well, I suppose so, but don't go making a habit of it. He should be up there with you in your room where you can keep an eye on him."

She bustled off giving the phone table a perfunctory dust, leaving Therese to ascend the creaking stairs, looking over her shoulder at her sleeping infant, and praying he would stay asleep until she at least pegged out the nappies.

It was some time after the washing had been done, her mother's letter had been read and replied to, and the newspaper had been scanned, that Therese descended the stairs to collect her baby. She could not believe that he had slept for so long, giving her a chance to catch up on all her chores.

But her happiness quickly dissolved into terror as, looking into the perambulator she discovered to her horror that it was empty. Someone had taken her baby!

Chapter Eleven

"Well, this is nice, Robert. Thanks for asking me."

Irene was having lunch at the club with Robert who had invited her at the last meeting of the AA just prior to Judy's discharge from the asylum. She had been unsure of leaving her sister but after telling Arthur of her conundrum he had reassured her he would call in and check on her while Irene was out.

"I do hope Judy will be alright. This is the first time I have left her on her own." Said Irene her fingers worrying the beads around her neck.

"I'm sure she will be perfectly fine, and your good neighbour Arthur is there to look in on her. Now, no more of your worrying. What do you feel like to eat?"

A slight smile crossed Irene's face as she perused the menu which Robert had proferred.

"The rissoles sound nice. And a cup of tea thank you, Robert."

"Very good. I will have the same."

The waitress came over and took the order.

"Now, that's out of the way we can relax" he said.

"Yes" replied Irene feeling only marginally better as she was still anxious about Judy.

"Well, how is everyone at the house? Have you had any new lodgers move in?"

"Oh, everyone is much the same. Therese, that young Irish girl I was telling you about, she had her baby."

"Oh did she? A girl or a boy?"

"A little boy, Danny, she called him. He's a pet. I look after him for a few hours when Therese works at the cafe."

"That's very generous of you, Irene. You don't find it a bit much now that Judy is staying with you?"

The waitress put their lunch on the table.

"No," continued Irene, "As a matter of fact, I rather enjoy it. Judy and I take him for walks down to the pier. I think the sea air does him good as he sleeps like a top. Also, Judy seems to benefit as well. I always notice her mood changing when we approach the sea."

Irene cut off a piece of rissole pushing some mashed potato onto it.

"Well, it sounds like it is a good deal all round for everyone." He said.

"Tea?"

"Yes, thank you."

He poured their tea and helped himself to three teaspoonfuls of sugar which made Irene squirm. She could not abide such sweetness.

"How have you found the new room?" he asked." Have you settled in?"

Irene had enlisted Robert's help to move her into the bigger room prior to Judy's arrival. He had also done some painting, touching up the walls which the former lodger Jimmy had originally painted. Mabel had been fussing around making sure they did not scrape any wallpaper off the walls as they carried the bed up the stairs.

"Now, mind how you go," she exclaimed, "I don't want the wallpaper ruined."

Irene thought how stupid that was as there were already sections of wallpaper which had peeled off and a bit more would not have mattered. It had taken quite a while to carry the bed as it was rather heavy, and the stairs were steep. The tattered carpet also did not help matters as they had to be mindful of the risk of tripping. Eventually, after a bit of pulling and pushing they got it into the room, and it was placed beside the bed which the previous lodgers had left. They, having decided to buy a new one as the wife had been left a legacy by some old aunt and they had money to spurge.

Irene had stepped back and surveyed the adjoining beds. She envisioned Judy and herself lying in them next to each other. Irene in a proper bed this time, and not the camp bed on which she had slept when she stayed before.

The next items to be brought up had been the table and chairs, and also the new rug to which she had treated herself. She had seen it in the second- hand shop when she had shopped with Therese. She had asked the salesperson to put it aside for her and had collected it a week later when she had saved up the money for the purchase. It was just the kind of rug she had been after and, although it had not been an expensive Persian rug like the one, she had at the big House, it had a similar cheerful pattern which she knew would brighten up the new room considerably.

"Oh yes, I knew the rug would make a difference," she had said when the rest of the furniture was brought in and she had placed a vase filled with daisies on the table. All that was now needed were some new curtains, but they would have to wait. The ones that were there now would have to suffice until either she bought some material and got Mona to run some up on her machine, or she bought some second hand.

"Yes, thanks, Robert, the room is certainly a lot better than the old one and that is partly due to your generosity, painting the walls, helping with the furniture. I'm really indebted to you."

"Oh, think nothing of it. It gave me something to do. I used to like doing that sort of thing when I was married. Painting or fixing whatever was broken around the house on my days off.

Felt it was relaxing after chasing robbers and sorting out drunken brawls, although it was rather quiet in Chester I must admit. There did not seem to be as much crime for some reason."

"Did you enjoy living there?" she asked as she put her knife and fork down on the plate, her rissoles eaten.

He sipped his tea.

"Yes, I did. I enjoyed walking around the roman ruins, and they have quite a good little museum run by a couple of local lasses. Have you been to Chester?"

"Once. The family I worked for knew the owners of Oakfield Manor in Upton and we all stayed there for a couple of weeks. I remember it had four chimney stacks with Tudor decoration. It was an enormous place, much bigger than my employer's house in Sussex. They had quite a lot of servants."

"I remember the old butler, Bartlett or Basset," she continued warming to her theme, "can't think of his name. Anyway, one day there was a cocktail party, and this butler was carrying a tray of drinks into the library and managed to trip over the dog. There were glasses and champagne flying everywhere with most of it soaking the gown of Lord Elsinore's wife. She went hysterical and demanded to be taken back to London."

"And did they go?" asked Robert eyebrows raised, ears attuned to the gossip, needing to hear more.

"They certainly did. There were maids and valets rushing around trying to pack the numerous suitcases which they brought. Lady Fotheringay, the hostess, was beside herself as now the dinner would be ruined to say nothing of her reputation! She was railing at her husband that she would be the talk of London and berating him for keeping on that doddery old fool who now had brought shame to the household."

"Oh, what a to do!" exclaimed Robert.

"Did he get the heave-ho after that?"

“No, he didn’t. Lord Fotheringay always had a soft spot for him as he had worked for his father. He was his batman in the war, but after the fracas in the library, they did not allow him to serve any more drinks. The footman took over and he was put on to light duties such as answering the door. They engaged a much younger butler to take over the role, but he did not turn out to be without his problems either.”

“What was wrong with him? Did he pinch the silver?” queried Robert thoroughly enjoying himself as he poured more tea into their cups.

“No, not the silver. I heard from the cook that he was caught in a compromising position in bed with one of the valets!”

Robert exploded in laughter spraying drops of tea over the tablecloth.

He took his handkerchief from his pocket to wipe his eyes.

“Unbelievable! The things that go on in those houses! You could write a book about it. I suppose he got his marching orders after that episode!”

Irene replied.

“Yes, they both did, and they were lucky the Police weren’t involved. The condition was that the law would not be contacted if they left immediately without any references, so they went off bag and baggage with their tails between their legs. I don’t know what happened to them after that.”

“Well, I’d say they got off lightly. The law takes a dim view of that sort of behaviour!”

Their lunch completed Robert summoned over the waitress and paid the bill, then they proceeded on their way back to Mabel’s where Robert would see Irene safely inside.

It was to a scene of disquiet that they returned. Mabel was on the telephone talking to the Police and Therese was sitting sobbing in the corner near the empty perambulator.

"What's going on?" exclaimed Irene going over to the distraught Therese and putting her arms around her.

"It's Danny!" she sobbed "We don't know where he is! I left him in the carriage while I went to do some chores and when I came back down, he wasn't there!" Oh, Irene, someone has taken him!"

By this time Mabel had completed her call and Robert stepped up.

"Have you checked all the rooms?"

"No, we haven't. Nobody living here is a kidnapper I can assure you" she bristled, "I run a respectable house. Someone must have come through the door and taken him. I told Therese here not to leave him near the door."

This put Therese into another fit of sobbing.

"That is as maybe. Now, madam, I am in the Force and I recommend that we check all the rooms before anything else is done."

"Where is your master key?" he demanded.

Mabel bustled off in a huff not appreciating being spoken to in that manner and having her authority challenged.

She hurried back key in hand, and they all trooped upstairs. The first room they came to was Arthur's. Robert knocked but, obtaining no response, he inserted the key and opened the door to find Arthur in is chair snoring loudly.

Irene went over to him.

"Arthur, Arthur, wake up" she said poking his arm.

He stirred.

"What, what the dickens?" he exclaimed as his eyes alighted on the assembly in his room.

"Arthur," said Irene "The baby's gone missing and was Judy alright while I was out?"

Arthur rubbed his rheumy eyes hardly comprehending what was going on.

"I was going in to check on her after I had a spot of lunch. Then I sat down here to do the crossword and must have dropped off. So sorry, so sorry. I'll go in now." He said heaving himself out of the chair now in a fluster.

"No, no my good man" Robert said assuredly,

"You stay where you are. Everything is in hand."

By this time, Irene had bolted out of the room followed by the snivelling Therese and Mabel. Fumbling in her bag, Irene withdrew the key to her room and opened the door praying that her sister would be there.

When they entered to their astonishment, they found lying on the bed Judy cradling the infant Danny and both fast asleep.

Robert came in soon after followed by Arthur, and by this stage Therese had scooped up her now crying baby smothering him with kisses and tears of happiness. Judy had also awakened to the disturbance and beheld the people in the room with wonder.

"Oh Judy" cried Irene putting her arms around her sister. "What did you do?"

Robert put the pieces into place surmising that Judy must have ventured downstairs when Arthur was asleep and seeing the baby left by himself in the carriage had brought him upstairs with her to mind.

Mabel scuttled downstairs to cancel the authorities, mumbling about letting that lunatic into the house, and she should never had agreed to it. That Irene should have left her in the asylum where she belonged. Turning the place into an uproar! If anything, else happens like this she will be giving the two of them their marching orders and no mistake! Never been anything like this happen in the years she had been in charge and having to get the law involved. It was too much!

After Mabel left everyone breathed a sigh of relief that both Judy and the baby were safe. Irene thanked Robert profusely for stepping into the breach and taking command of the situation without the need to involve anyone else of authority. She invited him and anyone and the others to join her in a glass of lemonade to calm their shattered nerves.

But in the end, it was just she, Judy and Arthur who accepted as Robert had promised to see an old friend who had just retired from the Force, Mabel murmured something about feeding her parrot and popping in to see the queens, and Therese had fled to the safety of her room to feed Danny and cuddle him tighter than she had ever done before.

Chapter Twelve

Through the smeared window of his room and the arrival of evening, Harry could just discern the pier of Brighton in the distance. He went over and sat on the lumpy bed. From the ceiling a naked light bulb hung dejectedly down from the ceiling which had decided to rid itself of paint, while the tattered rug strained to offer some warmth and cosiness, failing miserably in its efforts.

Well, he thought, they wouldn't think to look for me here, not in this dump. Probably searching around the swanky joints in London. He got up and brought the bag over to the bed. He wanted to look at the money again. All the pounds he had stolen from his employer, Mr Todmarsh, solicitor- at- law of Baker Street. He had smooth talked his way into the job telling old Toddy what he wanted to hear, that he was good with the books. It was so easy to forge his signature and cash the cheque. The bank was on friendly terms with old Harry the bookkeeper. Always a joke or two passing between him and that pip squeak teller, wet behind the ears, thinking about what girl he would be taking to the pictures that night. And that Toddy, too busy with his briefs, drinking and womanising, to notice what old Harry was up to. It was like taking candy from a baby!

A knock on the door.

"Hello, Mr Thomas, are you there?"

He quickly locked the bag and put it on top of the wardrobe then opened the door to be confronted with the landlady, Mabel Dawson with the red dyed hair and lips to match.

"Is everything to your satisfaction?" she asked "The view? You did request a view?"

"Yes, thank you, the view is good" Harry replied.

"And I forgot to tell you that you must put a shilling in the meter for the hot water. No more than six inches in the bath, and there is a roster. Does Thursday suit?"

Harry agreed on Thursday, anything to get rid of the old biddy. Six inches! Give her six inches if she's not careful. Bet she's on a nice little earner here. Pocketing the lodgers' money and not spending any of it maintaining the place. Run down dump.

As there was no wardrobe in sight, he put his clothes away in the rickety chest of drawers which smelled of mothballs and the odour of the former lodger's clothes – stale and of tobacco.

He went over to the mirror hanging over the cracked wash-basin-cum-sink. His eyes took in the small cupboard on which sat a grill and two small elements. Won't be able to cook much here, he thought. He passed by the mirror which had a crack running crookedly down the middle. He peered into it then straightening his wig and adjusting his moustache set off to see what Brighton had to offer.

Chapter Thirteen

"Hello Mabel" squawked Billy the parrot as he saw her walk in the door. After the episode with that lunatic taking the baby she had spent a couple of hours carousing with the queens who were in a sociable mood. They had opened a third bottle of shiraz and had insisted Mabel join them in finishing it.

Much rather be with them than having lemonade with that Irene and her crazy sister, she thought to herself. Those two are skating on thin ice at the moment. At least I have another new lodger in now so if those two go it won't be so bad. Wonder why he arrived so late? Oh well, better late than never as they say.

"You are a cheeky boy and no mistake" said Mabel going over to the cage.

Billy poked his beak through the bars and looked at her with beady eyes.

"Cheeky boy, no mistake," he replied.

Mabel staggered to the cupboard and took the packet of bird seed, then opening the cage, refilled Billy's bowl spilling seeds on the floor in the process.

"Damn, stupid woman" she swore and bent down attempting to pick up the seeds.

"Stupid woman" said Billy as he saw his opportunity to escape his prison and flew out over Mabel landing on the top of the cupboard.

"Naughty boy, come down off there!" she yelled.

"Naughty boy" Billy squawked back looking down at Mabel from his new perch.

"You come down here this minute Billy."

She tottered over to the broom cupboard and withdrew the mop then brandished it in the direction of Billy. He then decided to end his game and docilely stepped onto the mop allowing Mabel to put him back in the cage. Then she threw the cover over ensuring him an early night.

"There you go boyo. Home sweet home. Nightie night! And don't you go pulling tricks like that again, otherwise you can find yourself another place to stay."

Mabel now thought what she needed was a nice cup of tea to calm her nerves and to listen to her favourite serial on the wireless. She put the kettle on the hob to boil then took the teapot and put in two spoonfuls of tea.

A knock sounded at the door.

"Yes? Who is it?" shouted Mabel.

She navigated her way to the door to find it was the new lodger Mr Thomas.

"Oh, yes, Mr Thomas? What can I do for you?"

"I seem to have lost my key" said Harry as his eyes took in the room beyond.

"Oh, well, you had better come in while I try to find a spare."

He walked in.

"Well, sit yourself down then" ordered Mabel.

Harry sat on an easy chair covered in a lurid floral and antimacassars and watched Mabel as she ambled over to the dresser and commenced rummaging through the top drawer.

"Nice room you've got here" said Harry as his eye roved around taking in the surroundings, one thing in particular piquing his interest- a painting on the wall- a Monet if he was not mistaken!

"Ah, here it is," cried Mabel.

She shut the drawer.

"Would you be wanting a cup of tea Mr Thomas? I've just boiled the kettle."

"That sounds just what I need" replied Harry.

He had walked over to the painting for a closer inspection.

"Is this a Monet?"

"Yes" she replied filling the teapot.

"I was given it by one of my admirers when I used to be on the stage, original it is, so I was told."

Unsteadily, she brought the pot over and set it down on the table.

Harry sat on one of the chairs while Mabel commenced pouring the tea slopping it over the table and into the saucers.

"Oopsy, ooh, silly me" she twittered.

"I'm afraid I have had one too many today Mr Thomas."

"Call me Percy" he said.

"I'll play mother" he added.

He took the pot and pouring the tea asked.

"Been partying have you?"

"I've been with those two downstairs. They always lead me astray" she giggled.

"And who are these good-time-charlies downstairs?" he asked.

"Oh, they're a couple of queens. Been there awhile. I let them stay on. Don't get much rent out of them but have to help out old fellow board treaders, don't I?"

Harry withdrew a hip flask and poured a good measure into his tea.

"Don't suppose I can tempt you with another drop of hard stuff?"

"Oo, no, but thanks for offering Percy" she said fingers playing with an escaped tendril of hair.

"So" said Harry after he took a good slurp of tea "You said you were on the stage?"

"Oh, yes, I was. They were the days. Singing and dancing all over the place."

"I was in the vaudeville" she added fingering her saucer and as she did a big burp escaped from her mouth.

"Oo, pardon me!"

"Better out than in. Isn't that what they say?" said Harry reaching over and patting her hand.

Mabel blushed and drank some tea.

"Used to travel all over England, even to Scotland. Got to meet all sorts" she said warming to her theme.

"That Gracie Fields was a good old stick. Remember one day she were on the stage and her bloomers fell down. You imagine, in front of all those people, with the bloomers down around her ankles! What did she do but stepped out of them and kicked them off the stage! Well, that brought the house down that did. She got a standing ovation! Never been anything like it before or since!"

"Well, you have led an interesting life. When did you take over this place?" queried Harry.

"Oh, it must be going on ten years now. Doesn't seem that long. Time flies. The old music hall was on its last legs. Wasn't the same as the old days. Didn't hold the attraction like it used to. That's the way of it. Life moves on. I heard about this place from one of the stage door johnnies. As a matter of fact, he's the one give me that painting" her finger pointing to the wall.

"He must have a few quid" interjected Harry.

"Yes, he did. Had a big inheritance. Only child. His old man had a chain of hotels. Made his money from that" explained Mabel thoroughly enjoying this tete a tete with her visitor.

"Still see him?" enquired Harry withdrawing a packet of cigarettes from his pocket and looking around for an ashtray.

Noticing this, Mabel went over to the dresser.

"No, not anymore" she said, "Toby's pushing up daisies now."

She brought an ashtray to the table. It was green with "Beautiful Bournemouth" painted across it. It was one of many Mabel had collected over the years-souvenirs of the places where she had performed. The dresser was groaning with her collectables: thimbles, dishes, tea towels, all jostling for space.

"Want one?" asked Harry offering the packet across the table.

"Don't mind if I do" twittered Mabel sitting down again and taking one, face alight with flirtation.

Harry took a gold lighter from his pocket and expertly lit Mabel's cigarette. Then he lit his and settled back in the chair.

"Well," said Mabel drawing on her cigarette "That's enough about me. What's your life story then?"

"Oh, nothing much to tell there. Went to the school of hard knocks. Done a bit of this and a bit of that" Harry said, careful not to say too much.

"And what is a bit of this and that?" queried Mabel, flicking the ash off her cigarette into the ashtray.

"Oh, buying and selling."

"Insurance?" asked Mabel "I seem to remember you saying you were in insurance."

"That's right" replied Harry "Selling insurance."

As the smoke suffused the room he added," Now I'm looking for something better."

Harry had discovered to his delight, there was a 24 hour casino located on the pier. More than enough time to launder some of that money! He stuffed as many notes as he could into the pockets of his trousers and coat then, donning sunglasses, made his way there.

As it was early, there were not many punters about, only the remnants of the night before. Bleary eyed, with the look of desperation, they huddled over the poker machines in the hope of striking the jackpot. A big one, which would lift them out of their penurious state and into an affluent one.

Harry walked over to the cashier and pulling out 1000 pounds from his pocket, bought some red and green chips. He then went to the roulette tables of which there were two. One stated that the maximum inside bet was 5 pounds while the other was 100 pounds. He settled for the latter at which there were 6 punters all desperate for a win. He placed his bets –inside, straight up, which was 35 to 1. The croupier cried, "No more bets" and spun the wheel.

Come on, you beauty, thought Harry as he watched the ball spin around. Land on mine! The ball flew around but, unfortunately for Harry, did not land on his numbers. His chips were cleared by the croupier, but Harry was not deterred. He went another round sticking to the same routine, hoping that his luck would change but to no avail.

Bugger this, he said to himself, the table is probably off kilter so us punters won't have a chance! Fuming, he strode off to the bar passing by the blackjack table. Now cards is what I should be playing! He ordered a whisky and then cast his mind back to the days when he was in the merchant navy where his card game skills had been honed during times of inactivity. He had been accused of cheating on more than one occasion which had resulted in a brawl, Harry inflicting serious damage on his accusers, which resulted in a spell in the brig.

Harry, along with his two brothers had been raised by his mother after his father had been incarcerated for armed robbery. He had been found dead in his cell, presumably from a heart attack, which was what the authorities had ruled. However, as Harry grew older, he had his doubts about this, as his father had made many enemies inside, and it was likely that one of the inmates or the guards had done him in.

To make ends meet, his mother had resorted to prostitution. She had never been faithful to Harry's father, even during their marriage so, when he was locked away, she decided it would be better to be paid for her services to support the family.

On many a night, Harry would be aware of strange men coming into the house and going into his mother's bedroom. Go to sleep now Harry, she would say as she escorted another punter into her room. He would hear the mattress creaking and sounds which unnerved him as he put the pillow over his head to block it out. His brothers were a lot younger than he and slept peacefully, oblivious to everything which was transpiring in the room next door.

It was not long after the death of his father that his mother decided to marry one of these n'ere- do- wells. With his big beer gut and tobacco-stained teeth, Harry used to recoil from him whenever he was around, especially when he started ordering him about. Making him do the housework (which was woman's work after all) when he was supposed to be doing homework, while he and his mother smooched on the lounge beer in hand, getting more drunk and then more irascible.

It had all come to a head one afternoon when Harry had forgotten to buy his stepfather's cigarettes on the way home from the boys' club where Harry was learning to box. His mother had gone to collect his brothers from the neighbour who minded them until his she returned from her cleaning job at the pub.

"What ya mean, you forgot to buy em, ya bloody imbecile?" he screeched as he poked Harry in the chest with his fat finger, his beery, nicotine breath nearly making Harry gag.

"I forgot, didn't I?" Harry retorted edging away from him.

"I'll give ya forgot."

He took a swing at Harry but missed as Harry ducked to avoid the blow.

"Bloody mongrel, good for nothin'" he mumbled.

He again took another swipe but Harry's time at the boxing ring was going to pay off as he landed a good left upper cut onto his stepfather's jaw. He sank to the ground just as his mother and brothers came in the door.

"Bloody hell, Harry, what've you done?" cried his mother running over to the prostrate form who was beginning to come to.

"I gave him what he deserves, the arsehole, and I'm not sticking around here to be treated like a skivvy. Don't know what you see in him, the stinky old fart. I'm off and you and him can go to hell."

With that Harry had grabbed a suitcase and shoved in a few clothes and, to his mother's pleading voice, and the cries of his brothers, he stormed out of the house never to return. From that day he had lost all contact with his family and never knew if they were alive or dead. He always hoped that his stepfather had died and was sorry that he was not able to finish him off that day when he had knocked him down. Should have smashed his fat head in there and then!

He spent time living on his wits on the streets, eventually joining gangs who taught him how to steal cars for joy-rides, shop-lifting, and stealing the money from the poor boxes in the churches. He won many a fight which erupted when one of the gang thought he had been short-changed as the spoils were divvied out after a haul. He was street smart and full of bravado.

However, he always knew there was something better than this small time thieving and he wanted to see a bit of the world, not stuck in this backwater of a place. He remembered seeing an advertisement for the merchant navy on the screen at the pictures one day. Yes, that's what I'll do. Jump on a ship and see the world!

So, Harry, arm freshly tattooed with an anchor, signed on, and sailed out of Portsmouth harbour on a cargo ship with a Filipino crew, bound for all the exotic places he had heard about: East Indies, Algeria, the Congo to name a few.

He would be one of the first to scuttle down the gangplank whenever the ship tied up at a port. Then, ensconced in a seedy bar, with a harlot on his knee and a glass of rum in his hand, the lies would flow about his charmed life back in England.

However, after another stint of moving cargo around in the sweltering heat of Algiers, and living cheek by jowl with the smelly, moody crew, one day he decided he had had enough. He was in a seething mood, nothing was going right, and he had been reprimanded by the captain who, with his rotund belly, had reminded him of his stepfather.

He had stormed off the ship and headed to the nearest bar for the rum which he hoped would assuage all the bitterness and hostility welling up inside him. However, those feelings persisted as in a hot, dingy room in a seamy brothel, Harry's hands had squeezed the life out of the old Algerian madam.

The tanker was about to weigh anchor when Harry had scuttled back on board. He went below decks and found a quiet spot where he counted the dinars he had stolen. Silly old tart, he said to himself. Should have been more careful with the takings! As they drew further away from the wharf, and the Algiers coastline diminished, the pleasure of the killing was only minimally eclipsed by the pounding in his rum addled brain.

When the body was discovered and reported to the Police, the authorities did not show any interest in tracking down the killer. She was only one of the many unfortunates who met their demise in that particular industry, catering as it did for the nefarious characters who sought its services.

So, Harry had got away with his crime, and sailed back to England where he conned old ladies into dodgy insurance schemes, and one old solicitor into taking him on as his bookkeeper.

"No more bets please."

The croupier announced. He was now at the Blackjack table and surveying the cards he had been dealt. He had wagered a good deal of money on this game. With consummate bravado, he had peeled off the notes as though he was a high roller, winking cheekily at the cashier as she handed over his chips.

Now the game was under way but, as the time ticked by, and the sweat commenced to gather on his brow, it was becoming more obvious to Harry that on that Tuesday in March lady luck had failed to materialise in the Brighton casino.

Chapter Fourteen

"I say, watch where you're going!" exclaimed Arthur "You nearly bowled me over!"

"Watch out yourself, you bloody old git." responded Harry, as he stumbled past into the gloom of Mabel's hallway.

"Well, really! exclaimed Arthur.

He shook his stick at Harry.

"What you need is a good spell in the army. Sort you out quick smart. Learn some manners." He harrumphed as he set off to the Victory Services Club to meet his old mates.

Must be a new lodger, thought Arthur. Don't much like the look of him. Will give him a wide berth. If that Mabel has any sense, she will tell him to look for other accommodation.

Can't have types like him in the place, what with the ladies living there. Irene and Judy and young Therese with the baby. Cheeky beggar! If I was younger, I would have given him something to go on with. A good clout around the ears would teach him a lesson!

His thoughts accompanied him to the bus stop. He sat down gratefully as the walk had made his knee ache but fortunately the sun had appeared making him feel a bit better. He always looked forward to his weekly outing to his club where, over a few ales he and his old mates from the battalion would chew the fat, reminiscing about the old days and their time spent fighting for king and country.

The bus arrived and Arthur hauled himself aboard and found a seat near the window.

"Morning, guv" said the conductor "How far you going?"

"Oh, just a few stops, thank you" replied Arthur handing over the fare.

"Right, you are then, and good job you have the exact money. Haven't got much change in the bag at the moment."

He handed Arthur his ticket and whistling, went on upstairs to collect more fares from the other passengers.

He's a cheerful fellow, thought Arthur. Should be more like him around the place, not like that drunken sod who's moved in to Mabel's, or that ex-husband of Betty's. I wonder what's happened to him? Nasty piece of work he was treating poor Betty like that. Should have served a bit of time in jail. That would have straightened him out!

His stop approaching, Arthur pulled the cord, grabbed his stick and waited until the bus stopped. The conductor helped him alight safely farewelling him with a "Cheerio, chum, enjoy your day" and the bus sailed off down the road on its journey to Hove.

Arriving at the club, Arthur looked around for his mates. There were usually four who came every Tuesday: Lionel, Clippy, Bruce and George. He spotted Lionel at the bar. He went over.

"Lionel" he said.

"Ah, Arthur, how are you? Can I get you a drink?"

"Oh, yes thank you Lionel, I'll have a pint of bitter."

"Right you are. The others are over there" said Lionel pointing in the direction of a table around which Bruce and George were seated.

"I can't see Clippy. Isn't he coming today?"

Lionel paid for the drinks and accompanying Arthur over to the table replied,

"No, he's in the hospital. Apparently, his chest got worse and he was admitted last week."

They arrived at the table and Lionel put the drinks down on the table.

"Hey up, Arthur," said George.

Bruce greeted Arthur who sat down heavily putting his stick beside him.

They each took their glasses and toasted each other as was their usual routine.

"Ah, that tasted good. Just what I needed" announced Arthur.

"That's not good news about Clippy. Lionel just told me he is in the hospital" he added.

"No, poor old Clip. I thought that gas would get him in the end" opined Bruce.

"He hasn't looked well for a while. Last time he was here he didn't have a good colour and I noticed he was struggling with his breathing. We thought we might go and visit him today after we have a spot of lunch."

Arthur took another sip of his ale, "That sounds a good idea. We might even cheer him up a bit."

"How are things in your neck of the woods Arthur?"

"Oh, pretty much the same. That young Therese had a boy. Bonny little chap he is. Although there was a bit of a to- do the other day and I feel I was the cause of it."

His friends leaned in a little closer, all the better to hear what Arthur was about to relate.

"What happened, old sport?" queried George.

"Well, Irene has her sister living with her there now. You know the one who was in the asylum. Well, Irene was going out for a meal and asked me to look in on Judy to make sure she was alright." He took another slug of ale.

"And Therese had left the baby in the carriage downstairs near the front door while she got on with some chores. You see the baby cries a lot and so she thought rather than disturb him when she brought him home from the shops, she would leave him there in the carriage to sleep."

"Yes, yes, get on with it!" interrupted George.

"Give me a chance, well to make a long story short. I happened to have dozed off and, in the meantime, Judy had taken herself off downstairs, found the baby in the carriage and brought him up to her room. When Therese had finished her chores, she went to get Danny and of course he wasn't there. She thought someone had kidnapped him!"

"Bloody hell!" exclaimed Bruce. "Did she call the bobbies?"

"She told Mabel who was in the act of calling them when Irene and her friend who is in the Force, came home. He got Mabel to give him a key to search the rooms. That's when they woke me up. Gave me a hell of a fright, all these people in the room, Therese crying her heart out and Irene's friend standing over me. I didn't know if I was Arthur or Martha!"

"I bet you didn't, old chum!" cried George "Then what happened?"

"Well, I confessed to Irene that I hadn't checked on her sister. She flew off and found her in bed with the baby, both of them fast asleep."

"So, all's well that ends well, as they say!" quipped George.

"Yes, you might say that. But I still feel guilty about causing all the bother," said Arthur.

"I wouldn't worry about it sport," said Bruce, "These things happen and nothing bad came of it. Now, how about we order something to eat and another ale, then we can mosey along and see Clip."

They ordered pork pies and mashed potato and another round of drinks. Arthur told them of his encounter with the new lodger who nearly knocked him over and all agreed that a spell in the army would be just what would sort him out. He also told them that Betty was still keen for him to visit her and the family in France and that Irene was encouraging him to go.

"You should go, while you're still mobile" said Mick slathering his pie with tomato sauce.

"Do you good." He added. "Life's too short. Even shorter now that we are all getting long in the tooth. Look at poor old Clip. He won't be going anywhere now except to the other side."

"That's right. I agree with George" Chimed in Lionel. "You take Irene's advice and get yourself over there. I hear the weather is beautiful in the summer, nice and warm. Do your leg good. Nothing like a good dose of sun to lift the spirits."

They finished their meal and after another round of drinks made their way to the hospital to see their old mate Clippy.

When they arrived at the ward, they were told by the Matron not to stay too long as Mr Gorton had not had a good night and needed as much rest as possible. They went over to the bed on which Clippy lay, an oxygen mask covering his face helping him to breathe.

His eyes opened blearily when he heard his friends surround his bed. Arthur held his scarred, bony hand, the hand which had held the guns and hurled the grenades at the Germans from the muddy trenches of Flanders.

"Sorry to see you like this old chum," said Arthur "Can we get you anything?"

Clippy shook his head.

George said brightly, "Arthur here is thinking about going over to France to see the family."

"Yes, that's right, Clip" said Arthur "I might pluck up some courage and go. If I do, I might try to visit that little village. You know the one where you had your eye on that French lassie."

"Yes, she was a corker that one, wasn't she Clip?" announced George, "But that father of hers kept her on a tight rein."

"Wouldn't blame him. Old Clip here was champing at the bit for a taste of the amour francais, weren't you Clippy?" said Bruce.

Clippy's eyes lit up at the mention of that time he and his mates had spent in that tiny village, the place where in the hayloft he had tasted the pure sweet kisses of a farmer's daughter, before everything had gone to hell in the ghastly battles of the days which followed.

He tried to keep that memory locked away in a special part of his brain so he could draw upon it when he was overtaken by those other horrific memories of the war.

He remembered there were lots of Australians fighting with them and doing a brilliant job killing the enemy. They were good blokes, those diggers, as they were called, they all had a good sense of humour and a good camaraderie. If it wasn't for them the place would have been in German hands, no doubt about it.

As if it was telepathy, Arthur mentioned the digger he had befriended, the one who shared his tobacco and those hard biscuits his mum had sent him all the way from Sydney. They all agreed about the hardness of them, the way they had to dunk them in some tea otherwise a chap would break his teeth on them!

Arthur thought of the poor blighter. He had got it in the end. Struck down by a bullet to his face, taking off the back of his head. He often wondered how his mother had taken the news, seeing as he was her only child.

“I’m sorry, but you all must leave now” announced Matron as she swooped into the ward.

“Mr Gorton must have his rest.”

So Arthur, Lionel, George and Bruce said their goodbyes to their mate as Matron adjusted the mask, ensuring that Clippy was inhaling the correct amount of oxygen.

They made their way out of the hospital each one lost in his own thoughts about poor old Clip, if he would survive another day, or be taken from them. They farewelled each other with the promise of catching up at the club the following week, god willing!

Chapter Fifteen

After all the disturbance of that day when Therese had thought her precious Danny had been taken from her, Therese had misgivings about continuing to live at Mabel's. Although Irene had been a good friend and had helped her in her travails, she was worried about what more Judy might do. She might end up actually stealing Danny and running away with him! And that new fellow who had just moved in. From what Arthur had told her he sounded like a nasty piece of work-nearly knocking him over in a drunken state and being rude to him, and sniffing around Mabel like a dog on heat, he wasn't to be trusted for sure! Irene said she didn't like the look of him. She said there was something about him which was not right. No, the best thing she could do was to get herself out of this place and find somewhere else to live.

Danny was sleeping soundly in the drawer, so she made herself a cup of tea, sat down and opened yesterday's Friday newspaper to see if there was a room to let. As she scanned the pages with the usual news about politics, robberies and the ads for the latest home appliances, her eyes were drawn to the word 'Australia' at the bottom of the page. It was an ad inserted by a cattle farmer called Mick Davis who was looking to sponsor a girl with the prospect of marriage if she proved suitable. He lived on a cattle property in Bourke, New South Wales, and he would pay the ten pounds as decreed by the Australian Government, to bring her out on a ship.

Therese could not believe it! Here was an opportunity to take Danny out of this dump, see Australia which she always wanted to see, and maybe even have a husband! What would her mam and da say to that when she wrote to them all the way from Australia! That would get the gossip going and no mistake!

Headstrong and wilful, her ma used to call her, and this would prove to be the case as she immediately opened her writing pad and taking her pen commenced her reply to the ad:

Brighton
2nd November 1950
Dear Mr Davis,

I have just read your ad in the Telegraph and am interested in coming over there.

I am 19 and from Dublin and a single mother with a baby called Danny who is nearly three months old. He is a good baby and is very precious to me so if you want me you must want my Danny too.

I have wanted to see Australia. Is it hot where you live and are there lots of kangaroos?

I am sending you a photo of myself so you can see what I look like.

If you write back, please send the letter to Post Office Box 35, Brighton, Sussex, United Kingdom

Thank you
Therese O'Brien

She went over to the drawer and found a recent photo of herself which she rather liked and put it in with the letter. She then carefully wrote the farmer's address on the envelope and sealed it. She went over to see if Danny was awake and found him stirring, one fist finding its way into his mouth. She scooped him up, changed his nappy which nearly made Therese gag with the stench of it.

"Pooh! She exclaimed, "I don't know, Danny. For a tiny baby you do make a mess!"

"Now, we are going for a walk to the shops to post a letter all the way to Australia!"

"Would you like to live there my Danny, and grow up to be some class of farmer?"

Danny looked at her with his trusting blue eyes and just as Therese had the fresh napkin ready to pin on him, he let flow a stream of urine which soaked the front of Therese's skirt.

"Oh no, you naughty boy!" Therese playfully admonished him, "Now I will have to wear something else!"

She cleaned him up again and smeared some lanolin on his nappy rash which had appeared a few days ago then, putting him safely back in the drawer, changed her skirt, donned an overcoat and put the letter in her bag.

"Now, we are ready for the great outdoors, my little man!"

She carried him downstairs all snug in his bunny rug and little pixie hat, and after putting him into the perambulator tucked the blanket around him and navigated him through the front door and out into a cold wind.

The sky was leaden, and Therese could see the waves dashing themselves against the promenade as the wind whipped the sea into a frenzy. Even the seagulls were finding it difficult to fly in such conditions.

"We had better not stay out too long in this, Danny," said Therese as she struggled to push the carriage against the wind.

It took her longer than usual to arrive at the post office but she finally made it albeit with her hair looking like it had not seen a brush that day.

"Good morning," said the postmistress whom Therese did not recognise.

"Terrible day out there."

"Yes, it is to be sure," replied Therese parking the carriage at the counter.

She took the letter from her bag and gave it to the woman.

"How much will this be to Australia?" she asked.

"Australia? It will cost you 6d if you send it airmail" she replied.

Therese thought about the cost.

"And if I don't send it airmail, how much will it be?"

"Well, it would be half, but mind, it would go on the ship and would take about two to three months."

"As long as that? Well, I'd better do the airmail then" she said putting 6d on the counter.

"Know someone over there do you dearie?" queried the postmistress keen to know some gossip.

"Oh no, not exactly" she replied not wanting to divulge anything.

"While I'm here, is there a letter for Therese O'Brien?"

"That's you, is it?" asked the woman.

"Yes, it is."

"Very well, I'll have a look."

She went over and after looking through a pile of mail eventually found a letter for Therese.

"Here's one from Dublin" she said giving it to Therese.

By this time Danny had woken up and was demanding to be fed.

"Oh, thank you" said Therese taking the letter and shoving it into her bag.

"Are you from Dublin, then?"

"Yes, I am, but I must be going. The baby needs a feed."

Therese wheeled out Danny, his face turning red with the exertion of his crying.

"Won't be long Danny, and you can have your bottle" she told him wishing she had thought to bring his dummy, but with all the excitement of Australia had forgotten all about it.

She arrived home just as the first icy drops of rain began to fall and carried the bawling Danny upstairs for his long- awaited bottle.

Chapter Sixteen

"Looks like it's going to be a white Christmas," said Mabel as she encountered Irene putting Danny in his carriage, mute Judy alongside.

"Yes, it does look like it. I hope the baby will be warm enough," responded Irene wrapping the bunny rug tightly around him and arranging the blanket.

"Well, he looks well wrapped. You're not taking him down the pier on a day like this surely?" she asked eyebrows raised." I heard the forecast on the BBC this morning and they said there were going to be showers with a chance of snow."

"Oh, I didn't listen to the wireless. Judy had a restless night and then I slept in. I have been all sixes and sevens this morning, haven't I Judy?" This directed to her sister who looked vacantly back at Irene.

"Then," she added, "Therese raced in with Danny and headed straight off to the cafe. She seemed rather more cheerful than she usually is."

"Maybe she has found a feller," replied Mabel.

"Oh, do you think so?"

"Well, she certainly has the looks. Would do her good if she settled down with someone. It's a hard life bringing up a kid on your own. I remember there was a girl who used to be in the vaudeville, had a baby. She used to be worn out with working and looking after him. Mind, she used to travel around with the troupe all over the place, so I suppose that would have been harder than staying in the one spot. All the same, it's not easy."

"No, it's not. I feel sorry for Therese. I'm glad that I can help her out a bit."

Judy started tugging on Irene's sleeve impatient to go on her outing, as she looked forward to getting out of the house for a while and seeing the sights outside.

"All right dear, we are going now," said Irene saying goodbye to Mabel and manoeuvring her sister and the carriage out the door.

"Ta ra then," called Mabel closing the door and collecting the mail which had been dropped in by the postman.

She looked through the pile and noticed it was bills except for a flyer which was advertising a jumble sale at the local hall.

Might go to that, thought Mabel. Could do with a new vase and that saucepan has seen better days. She took the mail into her room and placed it on the table. I'll deal with those later, don't feel like looking at bills. It's all I seem to get these days, nothing but bills. The electric has gone up lately. Have to make sure no one is leaving the lights on around the place, and I still have to pay that feller who fixed the hot water heater. He charged like a wounded bull, and no mistake! Four quid for only half and hour's work! It's daylight robbery, that's what it is! Won't be getting him back here that's for sure.

This she said out loud, Billy squawking back, "Daylight robbery, daylight robbery!"

"That's enough Billy, you're getting too big for your boots!" she told him going over to his cage. She put her finger through the bars so he could nibble it.

"Good boy Billy. You like that don't you? Having a little nibble."

Finished with that he pecked at some seed, then flew up onto his perch looking down at her with his beady eyes.

Oh well, this won't get the turnips stewed. I'd better get on. Have to go down the shops later and get something for tea. Might get some beef from the butcher and make a stew, still got an onion and a few carrots left. I'll just buy a parsnip and put that in. Makes a difference, a parsnip does, and if I make enough, I will have some left over for the next day.

Cheered by this thought, she went to the cupboard and took out the bucket, mop, borax, vinegar and a rag, then tying on her apron sailed off up the stairs to tackle the bathroom.

She was assailed by a bathtub grey with scum, the drain clogged with the lodgers' hairs entwined into a ball all different colours. The sink was no better. Filled with scummy water, because someone had not pulled out the plug, it too had hairs although they were bristles, from someone's shave, and not the pubic and head hairs of the bath.

Bloody hell they're a filthy lot! They can't even clean up after themselves and there's no notice taken of the sign I put up on the wall: **'PLEASE CONSIDER OTHERS AND WIPE AROUND BATH'**

Don't know where to start first, the place is such a mess. She picked up the sodden towel and threw it into the corner, then collected the matches from the floor and placed them into the pocket of her apron along with the ball of hair which she distastefully removed from the bath. These she would dispose of in the garbage bin when she went downstairs.

She went over to the sink, pulled the plug, then wetting the rag, sprinkled some borax onto it and commenced cleaning. Then, with more borax, vinegar and lots of elbow grease, gave the bathtub a good scrub. Pleased with the result of her efforts, she turned the tap on and let the residue flow down the drain, then, getting up off her knees, which were by then as red as her hands, she wielded the mop over the floor. She had nearly finished when there was a knock on the door.

"Who is it? I'm cleaning the bathroom." She yelled.

"It's Percy. Just checking if I left my lighter in there."

Mabel quickly checked her appearance in the mirror. Her face was red with the exertions of her cleaning and there were beads of perspiration across her upper lip. She wiped them off with her apron, then, tucking a stray tendril of hair behind her ear, opened the door with a smile on her face.

"No, Percy. There's no lighter here that I can see, although there is a wet towel I found on the floor. That wouldn't belong to you, would it?"

Harry sidled in.

"No, that's not mine," he replied looking at the towel.

He noticed the cleanliness of the room.

"You've done a good job with the room, toots."

A blush crossed her face.

"Ooh, thank you Percy," she trilled, thrilled with his appreciation "I'm glad you noticed. It was such a mess when I came up here, I can tell you. I don't know why people are so dirty. I even put up a sign, and that's useless."

The tendril which she had tucked behind her ear had now again escaped. Harry came closer and, reaching over, tucked it back where it belonged.

Mabel's heart skipped a beat.

"Oh, I must look a fright. Like an old char."

Flustered, she turned away to collect her cleaning implements.

"Let me help you with those." He offered taking the mop and bucket.

"Oh, ta, that would be helpful, I'm sure."

The two of them clattered downstairs to Mabel's room where they were greeted by Billy.

"Squawk, daylight robbery, daylight robbery!"

"Stop that Billy, you talk too much, you do!" she admonished him as she put away the mop and bucket.

"What's he talking about, robbery?" queried Harry feeling a bit discomfited by this announcement.

"Oh, take no notice of him. I was talking to myself before about how much I had to pay to get the water heater repaired."

She took off her apron and noticing the ball of hair in the pocket she quickly squashed up the apron and kicked it into the corner until her guest departed. It would not be very seemly for Percy to witness an obscene thing as that when she was about to offer him a cup of tea.

"Stay for a cuppa, Percy?"

"Don't mind if I do."

He went over to the dresser and helped himself to the Bournemouth ashtray, the one he had used the last time he was here.

He sat down and as Mabel put on the kettle, took a cigarette from the pack and lit up.

"So," said Mabel sitting down opposite him.

"How's things with you? Have you got anything on the go?"

"Not yet," he answered blowing a smoke ring in the air watching it ascend and then disappear.

"Seen anything of the others?" she asked.

"I bumped into that old codger the other day. Bit grumpy, if you ask me."

"Oh, Arthur? He must have had trouble with his knee. I wouldn't call him grumpy."

The kettle boiled, she made the tea and brought it over.

"Biscuit?" she asked.

"Wouldn't say no."

She went over to the cupboard and put two biscuits on a plate then brought them over.

Mean old biddy, two biscuits!

"Did you hear about the ruckus a few weeks ago about the baby and Arthur and that mad sister of Irene's?"

"No, can't say I did. Been out a lot. Must have missed it."

"Well, that Irene had gone out and left Arthur in charge of checking on Judy."

"She's the one who's the picnic short of a sandwich?" he asked taking the two biscuits, dunking one into his tea and the other resting in the saucer.

"Yes, she is. Well, Therese had left the baby in the carriage downstairs and thought it had been kidnapped. Turned out that Judy had gone down and taken him to bed with her. Arthur had dozed off in his chair and didn't know anything about it until Irene came back with her friend and they found the baby with Judy both of them fast asleep."

"That'll teach that Irene a lesson." He said. "She won't be leaving the old boy in charge again and I wouldn't put anything past that psycho sister either."

Mabel sipped her tea and, noticing Harry had taken possession of the two biscuits, went and got another one and brought it over.

"No, you're right there Percy. I was thinking the same. Never know what she might do. Murder us all in our beds! I read about someone like her years ago. They said this person had some mind disorder and didn't speak but then something triggered him off and he upped and stabbed his parents to death with a kitchen knife! Makes me blood run cold just thinking about it!"

"So, what's your schedule today?" he asked, changing the subject. He flicked some ash into the tray and bit into the second biscuit.

"I have to go down the shops later. Thought I would pick up some beef and make a stew. You like stew Percy?"

"It's alright on a cold night. Mam used to make it sometimes, though it wasn't beef. She used to stew up mutton, but it always tasted greasy."

"Well, my stew never tastes greasy I can assure you of that! I always make sure the butcher gives me a good piece of meat. That's the secret. A good piece of beef and suet. If you're not doing anything tonight, you can come and have some if you like."

Harry thought about this. He would not mind a good hot meal. Better than braving the elements outside trying to find a decent joint to eat in. Not many classy places in this Brighton hole, and that wind would freeze the balls of a brass monkey! The old duck had better give me a good serving, not like those biscuits! Might bring in that bottle of red I bought yesterday. Get her nice and sauced. Think she likes getting on the sauce. Might even get her in the sack. Been a while since I've had any and might be a good chance to lift that painting off the wall and then skedaddle out of here with the left- over loot. That Irene has been giving me funny looks lately, she might be wising up. She's no slouch, even though that sister of hers should be back in the loony bin. Yes, I think it might be time to call it a day here, Harry me boy, and get going while the going is good!

"Ok, you're on. What time are we eating?"

"Ooh, alright then Percy," she trilled, "Come in about seven. We can have a sherry beforehand."

He finished his tea and stubbed out his cigarette.

"Seven it is. I'll bring a bottle."

It was both a mixture of surprise and pleasure which descended on Mabel as her backside was given a quick slap by Harry on his way out.

Ooh, he's like one of those Italian fellers, she thought. I'd better not encourage him too much. Might be more than I can handle. But why should I worry? Been a long time since someone has paid me any attention. About time I had a bit of fun. No harm in it. Now, I'd better make myself something for lunch and then get off to buy that beef before all the good pieces are sold!

She quickly threw the contents of the apron pockets in the bin, made a tomato sandwich and had some of the left-over tea. After having a good wash at the sink she changed her dress and combed her hair. Then, with a skip in her step, took off down the street, basket in hand to buy the beef with which she would make the tea for herself and Percy.

Chapter Seventeen

As another bout of sickness overcame her while the ship pitched and rolled, Therese was beginning to regret her decision to travel with Danny on such a long voyage.

They were on board the Fairsea halfway between England and Australia and this was the third day of high winds and rough seas. The corridors stank of passengers' vomit and mess decks were emptied of people unable to face the smell of food, while the nauseating smell of White King bleach made them feel even worse!

She had received a favourable reply from her farmer in Australia saying that she seemed a nice natural kind of girl, he loved children and, if everything worked out, he would love her baby as his own. He also said he loved the Irish and their accents, and his grandparents were from Tipperary so they would have something in common! He had wired the money for her fare with a bit extra for her requirements and would be meeting her at the Overseas Passenger Terminal at Circular Quay in Sydney. From there, they would take a taxi to Central Railway station and board a train to his property in Bourke.

Irene had been quite taken aback when Therese had walked in after working at the cafe and told her all about the ad in the paper, about the cattleman from Australia looking for a prospective wife to bring out from the UK, and that she had responded straight away and was excitedly awaiting a reply.

"But Therese," she had said "You don't know anything about the man! He might be a murderer or any sort of scoundrel."

Therese had countered, "Nah, it will be alright, Irene. If I don't like the look of him, I won't stay there."

"That's all very well, dear but where will you go? You'll be stuck out there in the back of nowhere in a strange land. And what about those aborigines? I've heard they're a wild lot. And little Danny. You have to be careful with him."

"I'll be careful, Irene," Therese had replied," I was talking to someone at the cafe whose daughter had gone over there as one of these ten- pound poms and she got on alright."

"Yes, but I'll bet she didn't go to a strange man's house in the back of beyond to be his wife!"

"I don't know, I didn't ask. All I know is, she's living in the country and is happy as Larry. She told her mother that the sun is so hot some days you could fry an egg on the ground! That sounds better than over here where we don't get much sun and it is nearly always cold and damp, and they are saying that we might have a white Christmas as well. No, give me some of that good Australian sun any day."

"Well, it's up to you, dear," Irene had replied.

"All I'm saying is please be careful and check things out. Make sure you have a back-up plan in case it doesn't work out. You might have to get a job and they won't be easy to come by in a place like that. It won't be like here where there are cafes and such."

"Have you let your family know of your plans? I'm sure your parents would be horrified about what you are considering."

Therese had looked down and mumbled she would write to them after she arrived over there, and everything was settled. She had felt guilty she had not yet replied to her mother's latest letter in which she had anxiously asked about the baby's birth, did everything go well, and did the nuns find it a good home, and when was she coming back to Dublin?

"Oh Therese," Irene had cried, "I really think you should let them know before you go gallivanting to the other side of the world. God forbid, if something happened to you and Danny on the way over!"

"And have you told Mabel so she can rent out your room?"

"I did and she was not happy about it. Said she would have to find someone else to put in there. She will probably charge them double what I was paying and wouldn't put a lick of paint on the walls. And the rug should be replaced. It's so thin and stained."

Irene replied, "Yes, the place certainly needs a good spruce up. It's amazing what a bit of paint does to improve appearances and a small rug would not set her back too much. She could buy a half decent one at the market. I've seen them there. Quite nice they are."

They continued chatting about how they would improve the house and Irene again reminded Therese about writing to her Mother before she left on her trip.

The words echoed in Therese's head as she wiped her mouth and lay on her bunk. She had heeded Irene's advice and had sent off a quick letter to her mother saying that she had changed her mind and kept the baby, and they were going to do a bit of travelling for a while. She said she would let her mother know when she had found a good place to live and she was not to worry. She could tell all the neighbours that Therese had been given some holidays as she was doing great work in the hospitality.

She remembered Irene at the wharf with her man friend come to farewell her. She had been told that Judy had been again admitted to the asylum for further treatment as there had been a few episodes of violent behaviour one of which had resulted in

Irene being cut by the bread knife. The Police had been summoned by Mabel when she had heard Irene's screams, so Therese had felt she had done the right thing and moved herself and Danny away from harm. There was no telling what poor Judy would do. Murder them all in their beds to be sure!

She looked over at her son peacefully asleep in his bunk tucked in by pillows so he would not fall out. There were no cabins as the ship had been converted from a troop to a passenger ship and the passengers slept in tiered bunks-women in one section and men in the other. Everyone lived in close proximity and there certainly was not much privacy.

She had befriended a girl, Louise, who was on her way to Melbourne, Australia. She had been a secretary in a legal firm in Bond Street, London and had broken up with her fiancé as, just prior to sending out the wedding invitations, she had found out that he was already married with a wife and two children in Glasgow. Her parents had told her she had had a lucky escape from this polygamist as they attempted to console her through the dark days which had followed. However, things had somewhat brightened as she had heard of the ten-pound pom scheme and decided then and there she would make a fresh start, and a new life for herself in Australia. She had sent her curriculum vitae to a few legal firms in Melbourne, one of which she had accepted, and she was to commence work in three days after arriving in Melbourne with Thyne & McSnape, Solicitors, in Collins Street.

Therese had told her of all her travails, the subterfuge, pretending to be in an unmarried mothers' home, the lodging house in Brighton, the replying to the farmer in Bourke. Many hours of boredom would be filled as, in fits of laughter, they compared their lives and their boyfriends, and discussed what life would be like in Australia.

Louise, who had little nephews, was also only too happy to mind Danny so Therese could have a break. When the sea was calm and the sun was shining, she would go on the deck and join in a game of quoits, or just sit in one of the chairs and let the sun wash over her. The Suez Canal had been beset by hordes of flies as the ship plied its way through, and the heat had been unbearable. It had been quite a different place at night as the heat dissipated and the searchlights lit up the waters, the banks giving the scene a magical aura.

When the ship had stopped at Aden, she even had a ride on a camel while Louise sat with Danny in the shade, as the dark-skinned masses assessed them, so pale did they both appear. After days of storms and gales sending most of the passengers fleeing to their beds, they were now enjoying weeks of calm seas and stomachs for which Therese was grateful, as she thought she could not cope with any more sea sickness. Danny had been fractious and off his milk and Therese had been at her wits end trying to keep up a supply of clean nappies for him.

There had been a few nights when the Italian crew organised entertainment with everyone dressing up. There was an Arabian night, a Wild West night and a 1920s night. This relieved some of the boredom of shipboard life and stopped fights from erupting often resulting in deckchairs being thrown overboard in the melee.

There were lots of non-English speaking migrants on board coming to forge a new life in Australia, and free English lessons were held for these people. Therese enjoyed hearing the Italians chattering away in their native tongue.

One of these Italians, an elderly Nonna, loved to nurse Danny as she sat on the deckchair next to Therese singing Italian lullabies while Danny looked at her with his questioning blue eyes. There would be friendly rivalry between her and Louise as they both loved to nurse the baby so they would each have a turn leaving Therese to have some time to herself.

"Bel bambino" (beautiful baby) Nonna would whisper "Vada a dormire" (go to sleep) and Danny would shut his eyes at her command. She seemed to weave a spell over him with Therese looking on and wondering why he would not do that for her: Go to sleep as if on cue. However, Nonna was experienced having had eight children and fourteen grandchildren, the latter all back in Sicily in a little fishing village called Acicastello about which Therese and Louise had been told in fractured English and lots of hand movements.

Finally, after six weeks of being at sea, on a cold and overcast day in July, the Fairsea sailed through the heads of Sydney harbour.

"Mother of god, it's just like home to be sure!" Therese exclaimed to Louise as they stood on the deck the wind whipping their hair into their eyes and Danny rugged up against the cold.

"Where's the sun? I thought it was always hot here?"

"That's right. It's no different, is it?" replied Louise "But" she added "I suppose we should expect it, as it is winter here after all."

Therese agreed, but was still disappointed that her first introduction to sunny Australia was a cold and dreary day with not a trace of sunshine. However, their spirits lifted somewhat when they caught sight of the magnificent structure of the harbour bridge connecting the two areas of Sydney.

When drops of rain started to fall, they decided to go below decks and ensure all their luggage was packed and ready for disembarkation at the overseas terminal. There was pandemonium as everyone rushed around gathering their belongings and talking excitedly at the tops of their voices. At last they had all arrived in the promised land and they, and especially Therese, were excited and apprehensive about this new adventure which was awaiting them, miles away from Britain in this country called Australia.

Chapter Eighteen

Clippy had struggled on for a week after his friends had visited him but it was on Armistice Day when he had drawn his final breath. Now Arthur and his mates were saying goodbye to him in a tiny church in the village of Iford in the South Downs, the place where Clippy had been born and where now he would forever rest.

Bruce had elected to say a short eulogy as he had known Clippy the longest. He spoke about his life on the sheep farm, where according to the stories told by his now deceased parents, he as a toddler tried to sweep up the wool in the shearing shed in wellingtons which were too big for him. Then, later on, becoming one of the fastest shearers in the South Downs. This feat had resulted in him being nicknamed Clippy, and the name had stuck through the years, not many people remembering that he was actually christened Andrew.

When Bruce had continued on about Clippy's time in the war, Arthur was transported back to that terrible time in France fighting the Bosch not knowing from one moment to the other if they would live or die. The trenches filled with mud and the bloated stinking corpses which had to be buried in the dark of night, while the Hun did the same with their dead. The rats which were as big as cats, gorging themselves on the rotting corpses. The shooting of these rats to alleviate the boredom which descended during the lulls in the fighting. The nits which got into the hair, resulting in the shaving of heads and other body areas to alleviate the terrible itch. And then the pleasure of cracking them, spraying the purplish red blood which you knew was yours. He thought of his blistered, cracked hands and how nice it was to take off his boots and waggle his toes in the fresh air now and then and rub on some whale oil. The constant digging in the mud to build the latrines into which you had to avoid falling. One poor bugger actually dying in one as nobody was able to pull him out. The terrible screams when someone was shot and the feeling of utter helplessness as they passed away before your eyes, the stretcher parties stumbling around in the mud and the dark unable to save them. He felt Lionel nudging him out of his reverie. He blessed himself and after saying a prayer for Clippy, joined the mourners as they followed the coffin out of the church.

As the vicar intoned the final prayers over the coffin, and Arthur and his mates had thrown some earth into the grave, Arthur spied some cow parsley growing in a crevice between some gravestones. He thought of his dear departed son Ned, who was not sleeping as Clippy would be in the bosom of Mother England, but far away in that Libyan cemetery.

In the last letter he had received from Betty she had said that if he came over Antoine might fly them all to Libya to visit Ned's grave. He had spent many nights worrying if he should go or not. He knew he was not getting any younger and it would mean a lot to Betty if he finally met her husband Antoine and their daughter Aimee. He had thought of that slip of a girl, Therese, getting herself and the baby off on that ship all the way to Australia!

I will have to tell them that I will be gone for a while. Mabel won't be too pleased about that. She will probably ask me to keep paying the rent now Therese's room is vacant. Well, I'll not be doing that. She will have to find another lodger.

He limped over to the parsley and, bending down, broke off a tiny bunch and stuffed into his pocket.

"Got some parsley, eh Arthur?" asked Bruce as he had seen his friend walk over.

"Yes, Ned used to like it. Don't know why. It's not like a flower," replied Arthur, a perplexed look on his face.

"Thought I would take some with me if I go to France," he added, "Betty always wanted to put some on Ned's grave if she ever had the chance of going to Libya."

"That sounds a lovely idea, Arthur. I remember you saying Ned loved the countryside."

They all started to walk away from the cemetery towards the village pub where they would have a toast to Clippy before catching the train back to Brighton.

"Have you decided yet to go over and see the family?" asked Bruce.

They had arrived at the pub and went inside.

"As a matter of fact, I have come to a decision," said Arthur.

He squeezed into the snug with George and Lionel and put his stick beside him.

Bruce said, "Well, I'll buy our drinks first, then when I come back, you can tell us what you decided."

He came back with their pints and they all raised their glasses and toasted their old mate Clippy, now in a better place free from his suffering.

"Now then, what is your decision old chum, are you going or not?" asked Bruce.

Arthur took a big slurp of his drink and, looking at his mates told them that he had notified his family in France he was coming over and as soon as he arrived home, he was packing his suitcase.

Chapter Nineteen

The headlines of the newspapers all screamed the same:

Mental patient arrested for landlady's murder in Brighton lodging house!

To Irene's horror, Judy had been arrested for the murder of Mabel and had been incarcerated in the psychiatric section of Brighton prison. Irene hoped to God that she did not do it but because of her recent violent tendencies she began to have her doubts. Her friend Robert said he would do all he could to help with the investigation and he would contact a good barrister he knew to handle the case.

Poor Judy was the talk of the town and Irene kept her head down whenever she went out which was just to shop for food. She ceased attending the AA meetings and was tempted back onto the drink by all the stress and anxiety foisted upon her.

However, Robert had stepped in and, with his support, helped her through the tough times of abstemiousness as he poured the sherry down the sink and listened as she sobbed about poor Judy's plight.

"Surely she could not have done it, Robert." She cried "I know she was becoming a bit violent, but surely she would not have strangled Mabel. She would not have been strong enough for a start."

Mabel was not meant to have been murdered that night. Everything was going well at first. The sherry had been drunk, the stew had been eaten, the piano played but when she had sidled up to him with the low cut dress, the crimson lips, and smelling of the same perfume his mother used to wear when the punters came calling, something had snapped in his brain.

Pushing her onto the bed, his fingers had wrapped themselves tightly around her crepey neck, the muscles in his arms straining beneath his skin in ropy cords.

"You bitch, you whore. I'll kill you," he yelled, "And my name's not Percy either. It's Harry see, Harry! You didn't know that did you, you stupid cow!" he screamed, tightening his grip as Mabel's eyes bulged, her hands tearing at his wrists trying to release him but failing miserably.

Billy was screeching and escaped from his cage as in the excitement of the planned tea, Mabel had forgotten to secure the latch. He flew up on top of the cupboard screeching, "Whore, bitch, kill you, kill you, It's Harry, it's Harry!"

Harry released Mabel and she slumped back on the bed; all life extinguished.

"Shut the fuck up, you bloody bird!" He yelled at Billy who was still sitting on the cupboard looking down at Mabel's killer. He dragged a chair over and climbed up on it then he grabbed the squawking Billy by the neck and roughly shoved him back into the cage. The shock of such treatment put a stop to his antics. Harry leapt down and grabbed the Monet off the wall. He shut the door and with the painting tucked under his jacket, hurried to his room where he packed his suitcase with his belongings and the left-over money. Then he went to bed in his clothes and the next morning called in to see the queens. He told them that Mabel had been called away urgently to visit her sick sister and she did not know when she would be returning. He told them that Mabel wanted them to look after the place in her absence and had left the parrot with plenty of food and water to last him for a few days, so they did not have to attend to him. He also told them that he would be leaving as he had to follow up a business deal which was pending.

He had then gone to the station and caught the next train to Victoria station, London where he boarded a first- class carriage to Dover. From there the ferry took him on to Dunkirk, thence to Paris and finally to Marseilles where he tracked down a disreputable surgeon whom he used to know in the days when he associated with such types.

In a seedy clinic in one of the backstreets near the harbour, Harry's nose was changed. He took a room nearby and waited for a few days until the swelling and bruising went down. Then, with sunglasses donned, and the painting stashed into his suitcase he made his way to Marseilles wharf and jumped on one of the ships destined for Cuba where other nefarious types such as he lived their lives.

Chapter Twenty

The rust-coloured land of Bourke with its many hills and gorges was now home to Therese and Danny. At first, she could not get used to the isolation of the property. There were no shops just down the street like there were back home in England, so if you ran out of something you could just walk down the road and buy it.

She took a while to get used to the aborigines, their skin black and their need to go on walk-about for some bush tucker. They looked on her and Danny like they were from another planet so fair were they compared to them. However, they all adored little Danny "Piccaninny" they called him, as they fought over who would nurse him under one of the coolabah trees on the property.

Therese and Mick had hit it off from the first moment they met at the overseas passenger terminal at Circular Quay in Sydney. She had recognised him in his big Akubra hat which he had told her in a letter he would be wearing, and he recognised her standing there beside a monstrous perambulator and surrounded by luggage. She had stayed overnight at the YWCA which was located near the terminal. Louise, the girl she had befriended on the ship, had also elected to stay there as she was not due to be in Melbourne for a couple of days. Louise was keen to have a good look around Sydney before she had to catch the Spirit of Progress train to Albury/Wodonga then to Melbourne. She told Therese that she was going to catch a ferry over to a place called Manly and was going to go to Kings Cross which she heard was like Soho in London, with strip clubs and the like.

Therese told her to mind she did not end up in the "white slave trade" to which she scoffed and said that if she had made it here with nothing happening to her, she would be ok. They had wished each other well and swapped addresses in the hope of keeping in touch.

"G'Day, Therese from Ireland" said Mick a big grin on his tanned face.

He extended his rough farmer's hand.

She shook it.

"To be sure," she replied," That's me, and I hope you are Mick the farmer from Bourke".

"That I am" he replied.

Therese pointed to the perambulator in which Danny was sleeping, "And this is my Danny!"

"He looks a bonza little bloke," said Mick.

"How was it in the hostel and how was your trip? Did you get seasick?"

"It wasn't too bad. I didn't get as sick as some of them with their heads hanging over the side, but I'm glad to be on the land again, to be sure."

"I'll bet you are, by crikey," he replied looking about for a trolley.

He saw a few lurking in a corner of the terminal and strode over to obtain one leaving Therese to assess how strong and masculine he looked. She noticed his way of walking indicating he spent lots of time on horseback. She remembered her Uncle Paddy who worked at the horse stables in Dingle used to walk like that as if there was something between his legs. He brought over the trolley and, after putting on the luggage, escorted them out of the terminal and into a taxi which he had summoned with a shrill whistle.

They were driven along George Street which Therese had noticed was choked with cars and double decker buses. They were painted cream and green, not like the red buses which plied the streets of London.

"Is the weather always like this in the winter over here?" asked Therese as she looked gloomily through the window now being streaked with rain.

"No, it's not. This rain is coastal. It should fine up tomorrow so the weather bureau says. Sorry it wasn't sunny for you when you arrived, but it must make you feel at home."

Therese sniffed, "But I don't want to be at home where we hardly see the sun and it's dark nearly all day in the winter. I want the hot sun you get here."

"Well, you will get so much sun when we get to Bourke, you will be soon wishing for some rainy days!"

"Oright, mate here ya are, Central station," exclaimed the driver as he pulled up at the kerb.

"That'll cost ya a quid."

Mick handed over the money and helped Therese and Danny out of the taxi. He then went around and extricated the carriage from the boot. Another trolley was located for the luggage and he escorted Therese and Danny to the country platforms. Their train, the Far West Express, was at platform 20 and Mick gave the luggage to the porter who stowed it and the perambulator into the luggage car. Then he helped Therese and Danny onto the train and within a few minutes they were off on their way to Bourke.

It took ten hours to get there, but by the time they had arrived Therese felt like she had known Mick all her life, so easy was it to talk to him. He seemed a kind, down to earth man with a good sense of humour, and had a way with Danny, nursing him back to sleep after giving him his milk which he had purchased from the dining car, ensuring that it had been sufficiently warmed first.

Over sandwiches which he had bought again from the dining car or at a station where the train had stopped, Therese had listened as Mick had told her all about the place where she would be living.

How she would have her own room with Danny. How she would be expected to cook for them as well as the jackaroos who worked for them. He told her about the red earth, and the night sky which was filled with so many sparkling stars you could reach out and grab them. He told her about the cattle which needed to be branded and drenched and the droving which would take him away for many days, and the aborigines who lived there and who liked going on walk-about. This Therese had questioned as she did not know much about these people only that they were dark skinned and lived in the bush. Mick had explained that they would go off periodically to hunt for bush tucker. He said that they had a spiritual connection to the land with the Rainbow Serpent featuring in their Dream Time stories which they told to their children. He said that there were many rocks in the outback of Australia on which the aborigines had painted these stories of the animals and birds which lived here thousands of years ago. He answered her questions about the kangaroos and koalas and if there were many spiders around as she had a fear of those especially those big huntsmen, the pictures of which she had seen once in a magazine. He reassured her they were harmless and were actually scared of people. That was why they usually hid high up in the corners of the ceiling and they were useful in keeping the mosquitoes under control. Still, Therese had felt herself shuddering at the thought of them creeping around and prayed they would stay high up in the ceiling right away from her and Danny!

She had asked Mick had he received any other replies to his advertisement, or was she the only one game enough to come from the other side of the world? He had told her that he had received three other replies together with photos. However, he had been drawn to Therese because, apart from her good looks, she had not advertised herself with "superficial charms" as the others had. This had been reassuring so, as the train clacked along passing through tiny whistle stops, she dozed on and off, not caring when her head dropped onto Mick's shoulder. Danny had been no trouble, sleeping between feeds and they both took turns nursing him on this long train journey.

By the time they arrived at the station in Bourke, Therese knew nearly everything there was to know about the Australian bush, as in her wakeful moments, Mick had regaled her about life in his beloved country. How it took only thirty-three days for a baby kangaroo to be born. How the baby was called a "Pinky," as it was pink, the size of a thumbnail, hairless and blind, and found its way to the mother's milk by instinct. How the aborigines were excellent trackers and were used to find anyone who got lost in the bush by following their tracks in the dirt.

The only thing which Therese did not know much about was Mick himself. He had not said if he had been married, or if his heart had been broken only that his mother lived at Broken Hill, married to Mick's stepfather, Bill. His father, Ron, had died a few years ago in an accident on the property when he fell under the combine harvester. Mick had indicated that he had been quite close to his father and it was only recently that he felt as though he was at last getting over it. He told her he had a sister who was a teacher in Townsville. She was unmarried and seemed to prefer it that way. She enjoyed travelling on her own and had seen quite a lot of the country when there were school holidays. As Therese slipped exhausted between the sheets of her first night under the Milky Way with Danny sleeping peacefully beside her, Therese was sure that in the fullness of time, she would find out more about this rugged Australian cattle farmer from Bourke.

It was on a Tuesday when the letter arrived, the postman flying in with it in a small plane like the Flying Doctor who flew thousands of miles to isolated properties to tend to the sick people of the bush. Therese had now been living in Bourke for three months and in that time, she had learnt to fry bacon and eggs freshly laid, gathered from the chooks which Danny loved to watch as they scratched around in the dirt. From the garden at the rear of the homestead she had picked the vegetables to accompany the steaks and chops which she now cooked correctly. Her first attempts had produced meat so tough they could hardly chew it, but Mick had stepped in and instructed her not to leave it on the griller so long.

Now she was a dab hand at cooking. She had got used to the old country stove which required wood to heat it, and now was in the process of putting some pumpkin scones into the oven for morning tea. Mick had gone on a cattle drive for a few weeks. She had felt lonely as he rode off into the dust, waving his big hat at her, shouting "Cheerio, take care of yourself and little Dan the man."

It didn't feel the same when he was not around, joking and cheerful. She found she was counting the days when he would be home again as they were getting along so well. Mick was pleased that Therese was not averse to mucking in on the property, feeding the pigs and helping out with the drenching and the tagging of the cattle. She even helped out at the birth of a calf, soothing the "mother to be" while Mick pulled the calf out of the cow by a rope. She could not grasp the fact that as soon as it had been born it had staggered to its feet making its way to its mother's teat for its first drink of milk. Not like a newborn baby who was entirely helpless!

They had gone for a couple of picnics down to the Darling river after all the chores were completed. Under the shade of a coolabah tree, with Danny crawling on the blanket trying to eat the green ants which had suddenly converged, Mick had divulged that he had had his heart broken two years ago. He had been seeing a girl whom he had met at one of the dances which were held periodically at the community hall in Bourke. They had been together for six months and he had thought everything had been going well but, apparently to his devastation, she had been seeing someone else while going with him. On the day when he had summoned the courage to ask her to marry him she had confessed everything and told him she was not in love with him and had been seeing someone else. This had left a bitter taste in his mouth and he was only now learning to trust people, women in particular. Therese had felt so sorry that this girl had led him on and broken his heart in this way. She had lent across and gave his shoulder a squeeze, and then had told him of the relationship she had with Danny's father. How he had used her to get what he had wanted and she not seeing hide nor hair of him since the day she learnt of her pregnancy. They both realised they had something in common in the "love stakes" and managed to have a chuckle about it. She could see that he was feeling more relaxed now with her and could also see that he would make a fine father, the way he related to Danny, tickling his tummy and talking to him like he was his own.

In Mick's absence, he had left a manager called Bob in charge. Therese got on well with him as he reminded her of one of her uncles in Ireland. He had the gift of the gab and a hearty appetite especially when the aroma of freshly baked scones wafted on the air.

He walked into the kitchen, the letter in hand.

"G'day Terry." He said. (He had started calling her that when he was first introduced, and the name had stuck).

"Here's a letter for ya. Looks like it's from Blighty."

"Oh hello yourself, Bob, thanks" She wiped her hands on her apron, then taking the letter saw that it was from Irene.

"I've just put some scones in the oven. They should be ready in about half an hour."

"Righto, I'll leave you to read your letter and I'll come back for a scone. Can never pass up them scones of yours. They're beaut!"

Bob went outside to have a talk and a smoko with one of the horsemen who was cleaning some saddles.

Therese sat down, shooed away a fly which had landed on her arm, then as Danny sat on the floor playing noisily with some lids, she opened the letter.

Brighton
January10th 1951

Dear Therese

I hope you and Danny had a good voyage on the ship and you are now both safe and well in Australia.

Therese, I have something very bad to tell you. Mabel is dead. She was found murdered in her room, strangled. They thought poor Judy had done it and arrested her. She was put into the psychiatric section of the Brighton prison and was in a bad way. I thought she could not have done it as she would not have been strong enough but as you know she had had a few violent episodes and so even I was beginning to have some doubts.

My friend Robert, who you know was in the Force, engaged a good Barrister to plead Judy's case. But it turns out we did not need such a smart fellow after all as you would never guess who it was that incriminated the killer. None other than Mabel's parrot that's who!

Apparently, it was that Percy! I never liked him, Therese. Remember I always said there was something not right about him. He killed her and then told Mona and Rita that Mabel had to go away urgently to see her sick sister and did not know when she would return. He told them that she wanted them to take charge of the place and that the bird was supplied with food and water. Well, it was a few days until they discovered her body, and the parrot was on his last legs as well. That Percy had shot through quick as you like. No one knows where he has got to and he took that painting of Mabel's as well. Probably gone to hock it somewhere or other.

Anyway, Therese poor Judy is now released from that terrible prison which would have been the finish for her I'm sure. She is under my custody now and is on a new course of medication which I am hoping will work.

But back to the parrot. Mona and Rita took him in with them. He took a while to recover as he was half starved, and that Percy mongrel must have injured him also. Well, they were both at the table eating some breakfast one morning when old Billy pipes up: I'll kill you, I'll kill you whore. I'm Harry, I'm Harry, not Percy!

Well, those queens high tailed it down to the Police Station to report what the bird had said, and the rest is history as they say. Poor Judy could not have said that. She could not speak at all! And calling himself Percy when he was Harry, dirty crook! Lord knows what else he was up to and who else he might have murdered in the past. The authorities are on the lookout for him, but I think he is well gone. They probably will never catch him; he was too quick for them. A conman was all he was and a killer to boot.

So, Therese that is the news. Sorry it was so bad, and I hope you are not too shocked by it. I know poor Mabel had her faults, but she did not deserve to die like that.

Let me know how you are faring out there in the bush. I hope it is not too hot and make sure little Danny is well protected from the heat. He has such fair skin as you do. I hope your farmer fellow is treating you well and if he is not, you get out of there.

Mona and Rita are trying to run the house, but they are not really suited for it. I don't know what will happen. I know it's a bit of a dump, but it's been home for me for many years. Arthur's room is still vacant. I'm glad he decided to leave not long after you. Good luck to him I say. Time is short and we must all try to make the most of our lives considering what happened to poor old Mabel. I wrote to him today to let him know what happened. He will no doubt be as shocked as you.

I've been seeing a lot of Robert. He has helped me get through all my troubles and he is good with Judy. I really don't know how I would have coped without him.

Well, dear, that is all the news for now. Sorry once again that it was so bad.

Kind regards
Your friend Irene
xx and a big hug to Danny
PS Have you seen many kangaroos there?

Therese sat with the letter in her lap shocked at what she had just read. She had not noticed the burning smell which was pervading the kitchen or that Danny was crawling towards the hot oven.

"Hey, where do you think you're off to young feller?" This from Bob who had just come in the door his sense of smell alerted to the burning scones.

He scooped up Danny putting him out of harm's way then, having seen the pale shocked face of Therese with the letter in her lap, immediately opened the oven to let out the smoke. He then took the tray of burnt scones and put it onto the table.

He came over to Therese.

"Got bad news, love?" He asked as he pulled up a chair and sat next to her.

Therese looked up and told him what she had read in the letter and then commenced crying about the scones which had burnt and what would everyone now eat for morning tea?

Bob patting her hand said not to worry her head about that. Everyone had had a good hearty breakfast this morning which should keep them going until lunchtime. The main thing was that she and the baby were alright away from that terrible situation back home in Brighton. Then he walked over to the cupboard and took down a bottle of brandy from which he poured a small amount into a glass. He brought it over to Therese and told her to drink it as it was the best thing for the shock she had received. She took it from him and swallowed every drop then, running over to her baby she sat on the floor, picked him up and held him more tightly than she had ever done before, the copious tears mingling with the red hair of his little head.

After lunch, and when Danny was having his afternoon nap, Therese went out onto the veranda which wrapped around the entire house. Through the shimmering heat the black crows swooped and cawed as she looked at the red hills, sentinels of this place she now called home. She noticed a couple of aboriginal women with their children sitting quietly under the coolabah tree to escape the afternoon heat, and she thought how lucky she was to be here in this land of droughts and flooding rains, far away from the horrific situation in Brighton. As a shiver went down her spine she walked to the kitchen and poured a glass of lemonade then, collecting her writing pad and pen, went back to the veranda. She sat down at the table and commenced her overdue letter to her Mother in Ireland. She had been putting it off for a while but, after the awful news from Brighton, which was bound to have been in the papers over there, she felt she should let her family know she and the baby were both safe.

Jindaroo Station
Bourke
New South Wales

Australia
May 16th 1951
Dear mam

Sorry I have not written sooner but I have been busy travelling. As you can see by the address, I am in Australia with my beautiful baby Danny. He is a good boy and you all would love him, I'm sure. I could not go through with the idea of giving him up to strangers. It would have broken my heart. I was living in a lodging house in Brighton where I became friends with a lady named Irene who helped me out when I had Danny and used to mind him for me when I worked at a cafe at the Brighton pier. She has a sister who got brain damage in the war and was in the asylum, but she had this shock treatment and they let her out to stay with Irene. She could not talk and was harmless and she liked to go with Irene on walks with Danny. She seemed to love my Danny. One day we found her asleep with Dan in her bed cuddled together.

Also, there was a lovely old man living there who had been a major in the war and he found me a perambulator on the street and fixed it and cleaned it up for me to push Danny in.

But I got fed up with living there and the weather being cold and rainy, so I replied to an advertisement I saw in the paper. This cattle farmer wanted a girl to come out from the UK to help him with the domestic duties with a view to marriage if things turned out. It was this ten-pound pom scheme that the Australian Government had brought in to get more people over here. So here I am, and I wouldn't change anything for the world. The farmer is called Mick Davis and a nicer man you could not want. He is good to me and looks on Danny as his own.

Now mam, don't think that there is any hanky-panky going on because there isn't. I sleep in my own room with Danny and Mick sleeps in his quite away from me.

I sailed over to Australia on the Fairsea with a lot of other migrants. There were lots of Italians and Greeks and I met another English girl who was going to work for solicitors in Melbourne. I didn't get as seasick as some of the others, and it was interesting calling in to all the places I have only heard about and did not think I would ever see. Mick was there to meet me at Circular Quay which is where the ships berth in Sydney. Mam, you should see the Sydney harbour bridge. It is a monster to be sure and there are trains and cars all going across it from the two sides of the city. Mick got us a taxi and we went down to Central Railway where the trains leave for the country. It took ten hours to get to Bourke and Mick looked after us on the way. He got Danny's bottles of milk warmed up and bought us sandwiches to eat. He is so happy and cheerful, and he told me his relations come from

Tipperary, so we have that in common. That is probably why he is so nice being part Irish.

There are aborigines living here at the station. They have dark skin and love my Danny. They call him their Piccaninny and Mick told me that some rocks in the outback have paintings on them which the aborigines did thousands of years ago. The dirt is very red here and when there is a dust storm everything turns red and the dust gets into all the nooks and crannies.

Mam, tell Nessie and Donal that I can see millions of stars up in the sky at night. I never knew there were so many and there is one that is so bright I call it my wishing star and wish all good things for you all abroad in Ireland. I have learnt how to cook and my scones are always a big hit around here especially with Bob who manages the property when Mick is away droving the cattle which is where he is now.

Danny is crawling now and trying to get into everything I have to watch him all the time. He loves to see the chooks when I collect their eggs but is a bit scared of the cattle and the horses but I hope when he gets bigger he will want to ride one. I love the sun here in Australia. It is so bright and not like our sun which always seemed to be weak.

Well, mam now you know Danny and I are safe and well over here I should tell you that there was a murder in that lodging house where I was living. You probably read about it in the paper. The landlady was strangled by one of the lodgers. An awful creature who said his name was Percy when he was really Harry. Irene the lady I told you about never liked him. She thought there was something about him that wasn't right. So it was just as well I got out of there when I did wasn't it?

That is all the news for now. I can hear Danny stirring from his nap.

Give my love to Da and big, big hugs to Nessie and Donal

Write to me and tell me all the news.

Your loving daughter
Therese xxx

It was after those few weeks when Mick had ridden in from the cattle muster that Therese had found herself running towards him. After he dismounted, she had thrown her arms around him so pleased was she that he had returned safe and sound to be with her and Danny so no harm would befall them. He had been quite taken aback by this public display of affection and was at a loss for words.

"What's all this then?" He queried looking at Therese, hair all awry and smudges of flour on her face.

"Oh, Mick, it's so good to see you. Me and Dan have missed you to be sure!"

They walked over to the homestead where, on the veranda, after a cup of strong tea and a slice of sponge cake Therese had related to him the awful news she had received from Irene. It was then that he had put his arms around her and as the red sun disappeared below the furthest hill their lips had joined in the kiss for which Therese had been hoping.

Chapter Twenty-one

"Another croissant dad?" asked Betty. They were finishing breakfast in the conservatory at Antoine's and Betty's house in Aix-En- Provence, Antoine's family home in Lourmarin having been sold as there was no suitable school at which Aimee could attend. It pained Antoine somewhat to sell his childhood home, with all the memories it had contained, both good and bad, but he knew it had to be done as Aimee was soon entering The Ecole Privee, the high school in Provence.

This new house was a bit more contemporary and much bigger and grander with plenty of rooms to accommodate guests. On the ground floor, Antoine had his study replete with bookcases groaning with books, a Turkish rug covered a polished floor and a fireplace produced much needed warmth when the cold mistral blew, and the snow fell. His rosewood desk was placed at a window which overlooked the garden and there was a splendid view of the alps in the distance. There was a beautiful terrace overlooking a huge swimming pool surrounded by overflowing pots of lavender, the perfume of which permeated the surrounding area in the summer months.

Arthur had finally plucked up the courage and gone over for the visit which had been made easier as his grandson Ben had decided to come with him. He had had some holidays due and thought it would be a good opportunity to also visit his relations and see some of France. Arthur had told Mabel that he would leaving a couple of days after Therese which had upset her. She had railed about rooms being left vacant and having to advertise for new lodgers. Irene had been bereft that all her neighbours were departing leaving her and Judy with just Mabel and Mona and Rita who she hardly had anything to do with.

Irene had kindly helped Arthur pack, ensuring he took all his warm clothes as well as his long johns to keep his legs warm, especially his bad leg which gave him more trouble in the winter. She had heard of the wind they called the mistral and how cold it could get when it was blowing. That, combined with snow, would make it even colder. Arthur had the wireless on as he enjoyed listening to the music which was broadcast from the BBC. Irene had thought the volume was a bit high but she realised Arthur was getting a little hard of hearing these days so she did not complain.

As she was packing his socks, she noticed a book nestled in among his clothes, and she had asked him if he meant to pack it or leave it out to read on the journey. He told her that he had inserted the sprig of cow parsley in the book in case he was able to go to Libya with the family and place it on Ned's grave. Irene had said that would be a lovely thing to do and would mean such a lot to both him and Betty. He had then retrieved from the drawer a little tin in which there was a dog-eared sheet of paper written by Ned from the battlefield in Tobruk. It had been among Ned's personal effects which the army had sent on to him. Arthur had kept and treasured it all these years and he would take it with him to show his family in France. He took it out and asked Irene if she would like to read it. She said she would if Arthur did not mind, and the two old friends sat down on the bed, the sheet of paper in Irene's hands.

Tobruk
Easter Monday 1941

Bardia attacked yesterday. Thousands of Italian prisoners taken. German infantry broke through wire defences with numerous machine guns, mortars and field pieces. Lots of our boys with terrible leg and stomach wounds from mines exploding up into the air. Hospital full of wounded and today 40 or 50 enemy bombers came and gave us hell. Hospital bombed and hospital ship too. The heat terrible. Flies pestering us all the time. Rats as big as cats, snakes and scorpions. Now shrapnel and bomb splinters falling all around us in the trench. This place is hell on earth. Nerves shattered. Can't take much more of this noise and the smell of death. Miss my darling girl and little Ben. Can't tell them much in a letter. Everything censored by the powers that be. No one knows at home what it's really like here. Better they don't know. It is all too awful to think about. Feel so tired like I could sleep forever but have to stay awake, so Fritz won't get me. Can't stop shaking. Can't take much more. Oh God, stop the noise, please stop!

There the diary ended, and Irene wiped away the tears which had sprung from her eyes. Arthur sniffed and averting his face folded up the paper, putting it back in the tin and secreting it down the side of the suitcase.

After he had arrived in France and received the terrible news of Mabel's murder Arthur was pleased, he was far away in another country. His family had rallied around and had helped him into a plush armchair near the fire. With soothing words of comfort and a glass of brandy, they had told him he could stay with them as long as he wanted.

As he had sipped the soothing libation, he pondered how lucky he and his fellow lodgers had been that they too had not been murdered in their beds. Never liked the bludger, ever since he nearly ran me over that morning shouting profanities, and Irene had always had misgivings about him. Mabel should never have rented him a room in the first place. But hindsight is always a fine thing. And poor Judy being blamed for it all! What a terrible thing for her and Irene having to deal with it. That parrot came in handy at the end. What a turn up for the books that was, old Billy saving the day for poor Judy! Don't think Mona and Rita would know much about running the place as Irene had said. Wonder when she was killed. I never heard anything, but then my hearing has not been the best lately. Have to find somewhere else to live if I go back. Wouldn't fancy living there now with all that has occurred. Good job young Therese got herself over to Australia with the youngster. Wonder how she is going? She would have got the fright of her life reading about what happened. Must write her a letter and see how she is.

"Oh no, thanks. I think I have had sufficient," replied Arthur patting his stomach and settling back in his chair.

"I will be as fat as a pig if I don't stop eating. I don't know how the French stay so slim with all this good food, and all the rich sauces and red wine. It's got me stumped!"

Since Arthur's and Ben's arrival in France there had been many delicious meals consumed both at the house and also at fine restaurants in the area. Arthur's palate took a while to get accustomed to the food as he was not used to such rich fare, especially the foie gras to which the French were partial. He found it extraordinary that wine would be served both at lunch and dinner. Even the children had a little wine mixed with water at meals. It certainly was not what happened at home in Britain that was for sure. Antoine certainly was a bon vivant and very generous to everyone.

At the most recent dinner at L'Epicurien, a notable restaurant, where he had taken all of them, after the goats cheese and apple tartines had been consumed, and over brandies, he had announced that they would be going to Libya in a few weeks' time. He would have completed his novel by then and could concentrate fully on the venture. Betty had thrown her arms around her husband and kissed him with abandon while Arthur, thinking of being able at last to place the parsley on his son's grave, had downed his brandy in one hit.

"What time is your friend expected?" this directed at Ben who was onto his second cup of coffee and second cigarette. Ben's friend, Kevin, from Bournemouth was coming to stay for a few days and he was travelling by train from Paris this morning. He was a chef having obtained a position as chef at the same hotel in which Ben was working and had been there for six months.

Arthur had noticed his grandson seemed on edge which he thought strange. He should have been happy having a mate to stay, instead he was like a cat on a hot brick. Can't work out these young ones anymore. Must be this old age. It's catching up with me now, what with this gammy leg giving me trouble and lately have been getting pain in the chest. Must be indigestion, all the rich food. Better not tell Betty. She will be worried and cancel the trip. Can't miss that. It's what she and I have wanted to do ever since dear Ned had died. To visit his grave, say a prayer and put his beloved parsley there. No, much better to keep all my ailments to myself.

"Oh, about elevenish Granddad," Ben replied. "I'm going to meet him at the station. Antoine said I could take the Renault."

"Can I come maman?" asked Amiee dunking her croissant into a bowl of milky coffee.

"Oh, I don't think so, ma cherie. Not today. Ben wants to have a little time with his friend before he has to deal with the likes of us!"

Aimee shrugged.

"D'accord, then I will listen to my new record. May I be excused, s'il vous plait?"

"Certainly, but don't have the music too loud. You know your father is trying to finish the book so we can go to Libya."

She leapt off the chair and tossing her hair, headed for the bedroom.

Betty called out to her.

"And Aimee, could you tidy up your room s'il vous plait, and don't leave your dirty clothes on the floor. They go in the laundry basket, n'est-ce pas?"

Ben stubbed out his cigarette and finished his coffee.

"Well, if you will excuse me too, I'll go and get ready, and say au revoir to Antoine."

Antoine was as usual ensconced in his study typing his novel, a Gauloise protruding from his lips, and the dregs of coffee in a cup beside him on the desk. A fire crackled in the fireplace warming the room. He looked up as Ben entered.

"Bonjour Ben. Are you on your way?"

"Yes, Antoine. I thought I would leave a little earlier in case there is traffic."

"Oui, that is best. The market is on today and it will be busy."

"How is the book progressing?" asked Ben looking over at the page in the typewriter.

"Ah" replied Antoine "Comme ci, comme sa. Having a little trouble sorting out the finis but hopefully it will sort out with another cafe. It makes the creative juices flow."

"Oh, I didn't know that. Is that why those writers used to congregate in the cafes in Paris?"

"Oui, that was so. That and the interaction of fellow writers, all how you say, having brainstorms?"

"Brainstorming" Ben responded.

"Oui, that is the word" replied Antoine. He looked at his watch.

"Well," he added, "You had better go if you want to be there in time for the train."

"Yes, I had better make tracks. Good luck with the writing. I hope it comes good."

Ben left Antoine mulling over the typewriter, then went to his room to brush his teeth and collect his coat. After checking his hair in the mirror for the third time this morning, he went to say goodbye to his Grandfather and his Aunt who were now in the kitchen washing and drying the breakfast dishes.

"I'll be off then."

"Mind you drive carefully" said Arthur, putting the tea towel on the bench. He limped over and gave Ben a hug.

"Yes, Ben, dear do be careful," Betty added drying her hands on her apron and coming over to plant a kiss on his cheek.

"The road can be tricky. There are a few hairpin bends, and it might be a bit slippery with that rain we had last night."

"I'll be careful, I promise. See you around twelve thirty. Say goodbye to Aimee for me. I didn't want to interrupt her when she is listening to her music."

Ben went out pulling his coat more tightly around him as the day was quite cold. He climbed into the car and headed off. Feeling anxious as well as excited to see his friend, he hoped his family would like him as he meant more to him than they would ever know.

Chapter Twenty-two

Judy was still uncommunicative. The new medication she had been prescribed had undoubtedly calmed her violent tendencies but, since her incarceration in the prison hospital, whatever spirit she had possessed had all but been extinguished.

On his rostered days off, Robert had volunteered to mind her to enable Irene to have some time to herself: To do the shopping, see a film, or simply to walk down to the Pavilion or the pier and enjoy a peaceful cup of tea and maybe a sandwich. She had been grateful for this respite as, up until now, she thought she would be unable to handle much more of the stress. She was now sitting in the cafe at the Pavilion which Arthur had told her had been used as a hospital in the first war, a great many Indians having been nursed within its ornate interior. Arthur had said that the Indians pretended they were Maharajahs as their domiciles at home were vastly different to this palatial edifice. She sat back and with a Devonshire tea before her, she thought of those wounded Indians and the vicissitudes of her life.

She dearly missed her old neighbours. Therese, with her funny Irish sayings and baby Danny, both of them bringing happiness to her humdrum life. She missed pushing Danny in his carriage down to the pier with Judy tagging alongside. She missed having a chinwag with Arthur over a cup of tea and hearing about his family over in France. Even Mabel she missed as she had been a big part of her life, taking her in when she had been at her worst, inebriated and dissolute, looking like something the cat had dragged in.

That had brought memories of Robert as she spread jam on to another scone and slathered on the cream. They had been walking out for a while now and her feelings for him seemed to be deepening. He had been her rock when she had been at her lowest and he had an understanding of the demon, alcohol. He had become an alcoholic when he had witnessed one too many deaths of children due to road accidents or abuse, turning to the bottle for the solace which never seemed to come, drinking himself to sleep to obliterate the terrible scenes he had seen. He knew how alcoholism was like a monstrous creature threatening to consume you at your weakest moment, then spit you out like an undigested piece of meat.

He had been wonderful with Judy, minding her so that Irene could enjoy some time to herself. He had even arranged for Judy to have respite care and there was someone coming from the Council this afternoon to interview all of them, especially Judy. Irene was praying that Judy would not be rejected because of her track record, the violent outbursts when now all that was hurled from her throat were screams. However, the medication she was currently taking seemed to be working, albeit slowly, so they all were living in hope of her recovery. Robert had mentioned on more than one occasion how he would like their relationship to be more permanent, but Irene wanted to have a bit more time for Judy to improve before she committed herself to a serious relationship.

Poor Mabel, her corpse discovered by Mona and Rita that morning when they entered her room to locate the money tin and receipt book. Their hysterical screams had echoed throughout the house, summoning the heater repair man who had come to collect his overdue payment. He had subsequently phoned for the Police who had arrived questioning the occupants of the house. One of the young Policeman taking statements, asking the whereabouts of everyone at the approximate time of Mabel's murder. Robert had been unavailable that day, confined to bed with a bad dose of influenza. The Police had estimated that Mabel had probably been dead for three days. After hearing of Judy's past history, and that she could not be accounted for on one of the nights in question as she had been left alone while Irene had helped Arthur pack, this had culminated in her arrest.

Mabel's body had been taken to the morgue for identification and forensic examination. Her sister Nora, whom Mabel was supposed to have visited was informed of the death and she had travelled by train from Liverpool to identify Mabel and attend the funeral, which had been held at the chapel of Brighton crematorium. Mona and Rita had gone to pay their respects, mingling with a few of Mabel's old friends from her days in the Vaudeville. They had all been shocked to hear of her terrible demise and there were many tears shed for the old trooper as they had called her. Irene, although she had wanted to attend felt she could not show her face there as Judy had been blamed for the murder.

After the service, they had repaired to the Brighton pub, where many stories were recounted of Mabel's career on the stage, singing and dancing her way around the country. During the course of the wake, it had been decided that because of Mabel's affinity with the music hall, her ashes would be scattered in Streatham Park cemetery, Greater London, the place in which former artists were interred. This decision had been related to Irene by Mona and Rita the next day after they had sufficiently recovered from their overindulgence of numerous libations consumed at the pub.

Having completed her tea, she paid the bill and hurried home just in time to tidy herself and Judy before the arrival of the woman from the Council.

Chapter Twenty-three

Dublin
June 23rd 1951
Dear Therese

I have not got over the shock of your letter. God help us and save us Therese I don't know what to make of you I don't. First you disobeyed me and didn't go to the nuns where you should have been and had the baby adopted instead you took yourself off to that terrible lodging house where all sorts lived. And bringing a baby there. You could have all been murdered in your beds. And that woman whose sister was in the mad house. A mad house Therese! And she was looking after your baby. What were you thinking, dear child of misfortune? And that old carriage that fellow found in the street. Lord knows what germs there were in that and you putting your baby in it. It's a wonder he didn't catch some disease. Well, it's thanks be to God you are all right. But your da is beside himself with the news and has taken to the drink again coming home six sheets to the wind tight as a state school. At least he goes to bed and sleeps it off instead of taking a swing at me. Of course, we told all the sticky beaks around about that you are in Australia now in the hospitality working in some class of hotel in the country. I couldn't ever tell them the truth. I could never lift my head up here with the shame of it all. It's better you are a long way away and no one knows what you have done.

You mind yourself miss with that feller you are staying with over there and don't you be having any more bairns before you are a married woman. When I get over the shock, I might enjoy being a grandmother to your boy and you can send me a photo of him. Has he got the red hair of that Dougal? I'll bet he has. He will have that fair skin which burns so you be careful and don't let him go out in that hot Australian sun Therese and you either as your skin will burn too. Well, I'm glad that you have taken to the cooking at least that is something.

I still can't believe you got yourself onto that ship with the baby and came all the way over the seas to Australia. There is no doubt about you Therese you were always foolhardy and stubborn. Took after Grandfather O'Flaherty abroad in Killarney so you did.

Nessie and Donal miss you and want to know when you are coming back, and they go out at night trying to see those stars you talked about and are sorry they can't see them brightly like you can. Nesssie has come on with the reading and Donal is not as lazy as he used to be. His new teacher Sister Stanislaus doesn't stand any nonsense and has given him a good walloping with the cane a few times when he hasn't done his homework or comes in late for class. I think Sister Regina let him get away with too much. He needs a firm hand does Donal. Also, Therese Nessie is making her First Communion next Sunday and I have altered the old dress you wore to yours. Magdalena O'Farrell is leading the flower strewers again. I don't know why the nuns don't give someone else a go. She is a favourite with the nuns and no mistake. Father

Hannan will be officiating and there is talk he will be made Monsignor in the not-too-distant future.

Mother O'Hara up the way has had her troubles. First that daughter of hers runs off with a married man, she was always a brazen huzzy was that Brenda, no better than she should be, then her eejit brother was arrested for drunkenness and lewd behaviour with a sheep at a farm in Cashel. A sheep Lord save us and keep us! The farmer caught him and called the gardai. I never liked that feller, had his eyes too close together. You can never trust someone with the eyes close together. I hope that your feller of yours doesn't have the eyes close together. I don't know what to make of the world now I really don't it's all going to pot to be sure.

Now Therese you make sure you still say your prayers and ask Our Lady to look after you over there in Australia and ask God to forgive you your sins.

Your loving Mother
Xx
Xxx from Nessie and Donal and your father

Chapter Twenty-four

The interview went well with Mrs Hutton, the woman from the Council. Judy had been on her best behaviour with no signs of violence. She had even managed a slight smile during the course of the visit. Robert was there to support Irene. Looking quite sartorially splendid in his grey suit and yellow tie, Irene could not believe how fortunate she was to have him in her life. She had made sure that the room was tidy, there were fresh flowers in the vase and the tea pot used was the one given to her for her 21st birthday by Lady Grimson, used only on special occasions.

"Well," said Mrs Hutton, "All seems to be in order. If you would just sign this form, I will be on my way."

She passed the form to Irene who then gave it to Robert to peruse.

It was a standard Council form stating that Judy's next of kin was granting permission to the Council respite team to look after Judy on the days stipulated. It also stated that there would be no responsibility taken if Judy damaged the premises and, in the event of any violent episodes, the team had permission to admit Judy to the nearest medical facility.

At the behest of Robert, Irene signed at the bottom of the form. She gave it back to Mrs Hutton who folded it and placed it into her bag.

"Thank you and thank you for the afternoon tea."

She stood up and put on her gloves, then, going over to Judy patted her hand and said, "Goodbye Judy. It was lovely to meet you."

Judy looked at her and another slight smile crossed her face.

Irene and Robert stood up and both thanked Mrs Hutton for coming and organising Judy's care. Robert walked her out the door and down the stairs and then came back up to Irene's room.

"Well, that's done," said Robert sitting down and pouring himself another cup of tea.

"Yes, what a relief," replied Irene "I was concerned that Judy might have had an episode, but she was on her best behaviour."

"More tea?" asked Robert

Irene nodded and went over to her sister who was turning the pages of a book containing pictures of various animals and birds. Irene had borrowed it from the library at the suggestion of her psychiatrist. It had proved worthwhile as Judy whiled away many hours poring over it and going back to the animals in which she was most interested. One of these Irene had noticed was a kookaburra, a bird found in Australia and it was this picture Judy was looking at now with a rapt expression.

Irene said, "You like this one, don't you pet? Do you know it is called a kookaburra and only lives in Australia? You know Australia, don't you? That is the country where Therese and Danny live. They probably see lots of kookaburras over there."

She left Judy enjoying her book and joined Robert at the table.

"You know, Robert" said Irene adding some milk to the tea "It was funny that the Council woman did not mention anything about Mabel."

"Well, I suppose she thought it was not appropriate considering how Judy was implicated. She probably did not want to cause us any embarrassment."

"Yes, I suppose that's right. I mean this place is rather notorious now. Everyone knows what happened here, there is no getting away with the fact."

Robert took her hand.

"Would you like to move out of here Irene? My place is not very big but I'm sure we could all fit somehow. Mind, you I would have to clean it up a bit first. Us single men tend to make a mess. We don't seem to be as tidy as you ladies, I'm afraid!"

"Oh, Robert that is a very kind gesture, but I would feel a bit uncomfortable living there with you. People might talk."

"Rubbish. We can't let other people run our lives, especially at our age. Anyway, you think it over. I am not going to rush you into anything. We'll see how Judy goes at the centre and then revisit the subject down the track."

"Yes, that is a good idea, Robert, let's do that."

Irene cleared away their cups and plates and put the tea pot back into the cupboard where it would remain until another special occasion occurred.

"Are you staying for tea tonight?" asked Irene "I bought some nice chops I could grill for us."

"Why not?" answered Robert. "I would not be having something as tasty as that. I would probably have baked beans on toast."

As the day quickly came to a close Irene drew the curtain. Robert took the paper and opening it to the sports section, sat down near Judy who remained entranced with her book. Irene took a dish and some peas. As they slipped from their shells, her mind was envisioning the prospect of her, Robert and Judy all living together under the one roof.

Chapter Twenty-five

Danny was in the Bourke Hospital after being flown in by the Flying Doctor Service. Therese had found Danny crying on the floor, with a red mark on his leg. She had picked him up whereupon he had vomited and turned pale. Therese knew straight away that he had been bitten by something and, if it was highly poisonous, her baby needed urgent medical attention. Mick was at a cattle auction and was not expected back until later in the day. She ran to find Bob who would know what to do but everywhere she searched he was nowhere to be found. By this time Danny looked as though he was losing consciousness. Frantic, she ran out to Alinga, the aboriginal woman who called Danny her Piccanniny.

"Oh Alinga," she cried "Can you help me? Danny has been bitten by something. Mick and Bob aren't here, and I have to get Danny to a doctor."

"You wait here Missy. Alinga get that medicine from the tree."

She took off out the door and soon was back with what looked like a piece of bark. She quickly made a poultice of it and held it on the bite.

"Now this one, he needs something cold on him."

They raced with Danny into the kitchen and Therese found some ice in the ice chest. She wrapped it in a tea towel and put it on his leg.

"Now missy, you ring on that telephone for that flying doctor feller."

They raced into the room in which the telephone was located. Alinga nursed Danny trying to soothe him with Dream Time stories.

Therese wound up the telephone and was connected to the Flying Doctor base in Broken Hill. She related to the operator all of Danny's symptoms and she was told to keep the cold compress on his leg, monitor his breathing and the plane would be there in about half an hour. If there was any major change she was to ring back and she would be instructed how to give mouth to mouth resuscitation.

Therese put down the phone and took Danny from Alinga then they went into the lounge-room to wait for the sound of the plane which seemed to take forever to arrive. Therese was beside herself with worry and kept praying constantly that the doctor would come soon and save her precious baby. She blamed herself for leaving him alone when she pegged out the sheet. Oh, why didn't I take him with me as I usually do, she questioned over and over. I am such a bad mother leaving him like that. Oh, please God make him better. Please make that doctor hurry up and come, please.

Then they heard the sound of the plane as it flew overhead and landed not far from the homestead.

"You stay here with Piccaninny missy. I go and get that feller."

With that she scooted off out the door and across the yard kicking up the dust as she ran, and it was not long before she returned not with a doctor but a nurse carrying a bag of medical supplies.

"Now then, let's look at him" she commanded.

"Yes, it's a spider bite all right. You didn't happen to see it?"

"No, no I don't know what it was. I was outside with the washing and I found Danny on the floor crying and the red mark on his leg." she sobbed.

"Well, it looks to me like it was a funnel web. You can detect the fang marks if you look carefully."

"Oh, oh, no not one of those. They are the worst kind. Oh Danny, please don't die!"

The nurse lay Danny down on the lounge and then took from her bag an injection which contained an anti-venene. She injected this into Danny's leg and because his condition was now deteriorating, commenced to perform CPR on him. Therese stood by horrified while Alinga put her black arm around her shaking shoulders trying to assuage the grief which was consuming her.

The nurses' fingers pressed down on Danny's chest 30 times then she blew into his mouth, then she recommenced. Up and down, up and down, blow, blow.

Slowly Danny's breathing returned to normal, and he opened his eyes. The nurse shone a torch into them to check the function of his pupils which she pronounced looked normal. She then told Therese that to be on the safe side it would be advisable if Danny was taken to the hospital in Bourke for observation overnight.

"Oh, yes, oh thank you, thank you for saving my Danny," she sobbed her handkerchief now wet with her tears.

"But I want to come with him."

"Of course but be quick. Just throw a couple of things in a bag for overnight and meet me in the plane."

Therese flew off and did as she was told. Knowing she must look a fright with her tear-stained face and hair all askew, she cared not two hoots how she looked as long as her precious Danny was alive. As she threw her nightdress and fresh underwear into a bag, she thought she had better write a note to Mick to let him know what had happened and where she and

Danny would be. She ran to the kitchen with her bag and found her writing pad. Quickly she scrawled a note to Mick and left it in a prominent place on the table, then, she hurried out to the plane where the pilot, the nurse and Danny awaited.

As the Beechcraft with RFDS on its side, took off stirring up the red dust and circled high over the homestead, Therese could just make out through the window, the tiny figure of her now good friend, Alinga as she waved liked mad at the plane.

Chapter Twenty-six

It was Thursday, and in two weeks' time Arthur and the family would be flying to Libya. Antoine had organised all their visas and everyone had undergone vaccinations to the consternation of Aimee who had a complete phobia of injections. She had to be bribed with a record of her favourite Jazz singer, Josephine Baker, which she then played constantly with the volume turned up, now she knew her father's novel was completed. She had quite enjoyed Ben staying with them as he was the only young person in the house, and she was glad that his friend was no longer there. She had been quite disconcerted when she had discovered the two of them in each other's arms kissing like married people do. She had posed this to Arthur one day when they were together in the library, she working on a jig-saw puzzle and he reading his book, War and Peace which he was finding rather onerous.

"Grandpere" she said.

"Yes, my dear" replied Arthur putting his bookmark on the page he was reading.

"Why do some men kiss like married people?"

Arthur unprepared for this question closed the book and took a few seconds to reply.

"Why do you want to know that?"

"Well, I saw Ben and his friend doing it."

Arthur rubbed his chin quite taken aback by this revelation. He had a suspicion that Ben's relationship with his friend might have been more than platonic, now this had just confirmed it.

"Oh, I expect they were probably just playing games, cherie."

Aimee went back to her puzzle content with Arthur's answer, while Arthur was left to worry about his grandson who, if he was found out to be a homosexual, would be dealt with in a severe way by the authorities back in England. Here in France, they had a more laissez-faire attitude to sexual proclivity, and mostly turned a blind eye to it as long as it was behind closed doors and not in public. Poor Ben. He certainly had had a terrible time of it when he was a lad. He deserves to have some joy in his life. Suppose we must embrace love wherever we can find it.

The aromas from the kitchen drifted into the room drawing Arthur away from his ruminations. He detected what might be a chicken stuffed with lemon, one of his favourite dishes and he salivated at the thought. Must try not to eat too much tonight. Been eating too much lately. Will forgo the after- dinner brandy too. Antoine loves his brandy. The French certainly enjoy their food and their liquor. Wonder what the food will be like in Libya. Probably be lots of those chickpeas and couscous. Not a fan of those peas. Give me wind, couscous isn't too bad though.

He was soon dozing in his chair, dreaming about roasted chickens which looked like rats. Star shells burst in the sky while the rotting soldiers' corpses mixed with the remains of dead horses. He could hear the lullabies sung by the Bosch as the bayonets were thrust into the enemy's stomachs and the upper-class girls driving not ambulances, but trucks filled with the bones of the dead so many they kept falling out onto the mud. He dreamed of Clippy gassed in the trench with shorn bloody sheep all around him.

"Grandpere, reveillez-vous," cried Aimee "Wake up, it's time for diner!"

Arthur stirred and awoke pleased to find himself and Aimee safe in Betty's house. She had his book in her hand and also the bunch of the dried cow parsley which had both fallen from his lap as he was sleeping.

"You dropped your book, Grandpere, and this." She handed Arthur the book and the parsley. He thanked her and to her question about the parsley explained that he was going to put it on Ned's grave when they all went to Libya.

She helped Arthur from the chair and gave him his stick, then escorted him into the dining room where Ben was helping Betty bring the dishes of vegetables from the kitchen. The chicken was already on the table waiting to be carved by Antoine who stood, knife at the ready.

Arthur sat down next to Aimee.

"This looks delicious, Betty." said Arthur.

"Thank you, Dad. But I had a lot of help from Ben."

"Well, thank you Ben" Arthur added.

Antoine carved the chicken.

"Aimerais-tu, would you like the drumstick or the breast Arthur?" asked Antoine.

"Oh, I'll have a little of the breast, merci Antoine, and not too many potatoes. I have been eating too much lately I fear."

They were now all assembled and Antoine opened the bottle of burgundy, pouring them all a glass, adding water to Aimee's.

"Sante," announced Antoine as they all clinked glasses.

They commenced eating and discussing the forthcoming trip to Libya. Aimee mentioned that Grandpere had some dried parsley in his book, and he was going to put it on the grave. Betty told Aimee she had wished that for many years and now it was actually going to happen. All the family at last going to Libya to visit Ned's grave. Antoine had bought Aimee a book about Libya, and she had spent time reading and learning about the war and the battle of Tobruk in which Ned had fought.

Ben told them that his friend, Kevin conveyed his thanks for making him feel welcome and that he had settled back into work at the hotel. Aimee asked Ben why did he play those kissing games with him when he was here, which prompted Arthur to spill his wine, the red stain spreading over the white damask tablecloth putting a halt to conversation. Ben had leapt from his chair to hunt down the salt, sprinkling it liberally over the stain in the hope of extinguishing both it and any resumption of the previous discussion.

The dinner resumed without any more discussion of sensitive subjects and, after the chocolate gateau, which Arthur could not resist, and coffee were consumed, Arthur announced that he would have an early night. He had felt the pain in his chest again during dinner and admonished himself for eating the cake. It was too rich, all that chocolate. He climbed into bed after drinking a glass of Alka Seltzer hoping that it would settle his indigestion. War and Peace lay on his bedside table but, as he reached across to retrieve it, a vice-like pain suddenly gripped his chest, and the book was knocked to the floor.

As the family finished their brandies and tidied the kitchen downstairs, Arthur's cries went unheeded. But then they stopped as Ned appeared in his soldier's uniform and beckoned his father to come with him towards the everlasting light.

Chapter Twenty-seven

Jindaroo Station
Bourke
October 1951
Dear Irene

I received your letter and sorry I have taken so long to reply to you. I was shocked about what happened to Mabel. That awful Percy creature. You always said there was something not right about him and you were right about that Irene. It gives me the creeps sure it does, knowing that there was a murderer in the house. Thanks be to God we are all safe. I wonder where he got to and if the Police ever find him and fancy taking Mabel's painting. He would get a good price for that on the black market and no mistake.

I am glad Robert is good to you and I hope Judy is improving on that new medication. Sure, they are always coming up with new treatments for people like her.

Irene, I have some good news to tell you. Mick has asked me to marry him. I am so happy. He is such a kind beautiful man and he loves my Danny like his own. He has such a good sense of humour and we make each other laugh. He proposed to me at his most favourite place which was a beautiful water hole surrounded by ferns. He called it his secret little oasis in the desert. He had packed a bottle of sparkling wine and some sandwiches into a picnic basket and we walked there late in the afternoon before the sun was setting. My friend Alinga minded Danny so we were able to have some time there together just the two of us. It was so romantic Irene. First, we had a swim in the cool water (Mick told me to wear a swimming costume). I thought we were going to the river when he said that. Then we sat on the blanket and ate our picnic and after that he asked me to marry him as the sun set behind the red hills. Of course, I said yes. I love living here in these wide-open spaces, where you can see the stars so clear at night you can almost touch them. And I love the sun and all the animals. There are so many Irene. Kangaroos with their joeys in their pouches, and the dogs which are always with the aborigines. They are lovely people too once you get to know them. At first, I was a bit scared of them when I arrived but now they are my friends especially Alinga. She helped me when little Dan was bitten by a funnel web spider. Sure, it was terrible, Irene. I was beside myself with worry. We had to ring for the flying doctor who came bringing a nurse and she knew Danny had been bitten by a funnel web as he had the red fang marks on his little leg. She had to give him some anti-venene injection and mouth to mouth resuscitation as he was unconscious for a while. Then we flew to the Bourke hospital in the plane. I had to leave Mick a note to tell him where we were as he was at a cattle auction and there was no one else around except Alinga to help me. Sure, I was glad she was there Irene. I was in such a panic. She got some bark from the tree which is what the aborigines use for spider bite and told me to put something cold on his leg, and to ring for the flying doctor. Anyway, Danny got on alright thank the Lord. He was put in the hospital for the observation, and we came home the next day. Mick was so pleased to see us. He was outside waiting for the plane to arrive and when we got out of the plane, he put his arms around us and I could see a tear falling down his cheek as he gave me a kiss right there for the pilot to see. But I couldn't care, I was so happy to be back home with my Danny safe and sound and with Mick. Sure, I didn't breathe a word of all that to ma. I am in enough trouble as it is. She already thinks it is a dangerous country to live.

I am quite a good cook now Irene as I have to cook for us and the station hands who live on the property. My scones are rated quite highly especially by Bob who is the manager when Mick is away droving the cattle. And I can bake a nice leg of lamb. The animals are killed on the property so there is never a shortage of good meat to eat. At first, I didn't like the idea of killing the animals and chooks so we could eat them but that is what happens here in the country and now I have got used to it and it doesn't worry me. Mind, I couldn't wring a chook's neck or kill a sheep myself that would be too terrible.

Now Irene, if Judy keeps improving and your Robert agrees I would love for you all to come here for our wedding. My family won't come. Ma wrote and told me that da has not been well. His chest has been playing up and I don't think he has forgiven me for having Danny and scooting off here. I know it is a long way, Irene, and is expensive but you could always do what I did and come here on that scheme of the Government. It is a beautiful country here Irene. Much better than over there where it is always damp, and people are snobby. Here everyone is equal and so friendly, and they call each other mate. They say, how you goin' mate alright? They don't talk like that over there in England that's for sure. And you don't have to live way out in the country like me you could live in Sydney or Melbourne, but that gets a bit cold, or Brisbane which is up north and is usually warm or Cairns which is further up and is always hot. That might suit you.

We are planning to have the wedding in December before Christmas. Just think Irene, you would not have to be over there in the freezing cold and I'm sure it would be just the tonic for Judy. They say that people who do not get much sunlight tend to be depressed. Anyway,

Irene let me know what you think. There is plenty of room for you all to stay at the homestead and you can see how my Danny has grown. You would not know him to be sure. He is turning into a little dinkum Aussie and with his red hair people are calling him Blue which is what they call males with red hair over here. When I take him with Mick into town, he is always the centre of attention everyone stopping us in the street to admire him and chuck him under the chin. The lady who serves us in the general store is called Flossie and when we go there, she always wants to have a nurse of him. She is a funny one. Wears her grey hair always pulled up in a bun, red rouge on the cheeks and lipstick to match. Sure, she must be about 90 years old, Irene. And every time we come in the shop she always comments about the weather. She says, "Turned out nice again." We only go to town once a month as it is too far to travel. It takes us three hours there and three hours back. We make a list of the supplies we need and there is a big freezer where we put the food, so it won't go off. It took me a while to get used to not having shops handy but now it is normal for me. It's funny Irene what you can get used to.

Well, that is all my news for now. Must get on and peel the potatoes for lunch or I'll get the sack.

Love from
Your friend Therese xx
Xx to Judy and your Robert
PS have you heard from Arthur?

Irene sat back in the chair. Through the window she noticed the sky grey as a bruise. It was raining again and lately she was feeling twinges of rheumatism in her fingers. She looked around the room. There was really nothing very cheerful about it apart from the painted walls and, since poor old Mabel had died, the house seemed to have a bad vibe.

Lately Irene had been giving some thought about her relationship with Robert. She knew he was a good person and would look after her and Judy. She had thought about his idea of moving into his place, but from what she had seen of it, there was no way they could all fit there. Men don't know much about the logistics of accommodating three adults in a comfortable manner. And the stuff he had there! Big, heavy furniture inherited from his mother, and knick knacks all jostling for space, requiring lots of dusting. No, it would not be possible to live there. Maybe Therese's suggestion was a good one. Maybe it would be the catalyst for all of them to make a fresh start over there in Australia. Therese seemed to have settled down, and she certainly made it sound like it was the land of milk and honey, but you could not believe all Therese says. She had a habit of embroidering the facts making things sound better than they were, but all the same, it might be worth considering. Lots of English people were going over there. What was to stop her, dear Judy and Robert from joining them? Nothing ventured, nothing gained, and it might do Judy good, as Therese said, to get more sun and have a complete change of scenery.

Today, Judy was in respite care and, as it was Robert's day off, he had gone to the dentist to have one of his molars checked. They had planned to see a film afterwards, and Irene was meeting him at the theatre after his appointment. She was looking forward to seeing this film, "All About Eve". It starred Bette Davis and Anne Baxter both nominated for Best Actress Awards. Irene loved going to see films. They were a great diversion, transporting her into another world, away from the memories of her past life and the worry about her sister. After the film, they would have a cup of tea and cake at the cafe near the theatre. It would be there Irene would broach Therese's suggestion of their possible move to Australia.

Chapter Twenty-eight

It was the next morning when Arthur had not appeared for breakfast that Betty had discovered his cold lifeless body. She had recoiled in horror, her screams bringing Antoine and Ben running into the room. Aimee was taking a bath at the time, so she was not confronted with the sight of her grandpere dead in his bed.

Antoine had gone over and gently closed Arthur's eyelids, and pulled up the sheet to his chin. He picked up the book and the sprig of parsley and put them on the bedside table as Betty, consumed with grief, laid her head on her father's chest soaking the sheet with her tears.

The priest and the local doctor were subsequently called. The former intoning the prayers of the dead and the latter writing a certificate of death. Aimee was told of her grandpere's passing and, although she was sad, she knew that he was an old man with ailments and that his time had come. She was more concerned about the cancellation of the journey to Libya and the parsley sprig which would not be taken to Ned's grave.

A family conference was held that night after Arthur's body had been transported to the funeral home in Aix En Provence. It was agreed by all that as it had been Betty's and Arthur's wish to go to Libya, and that as Arthur had carried with him the parsley all the way from England to France, they would still go on the planned journey.

In the short time they had before their departure, Antoine had arranged a beautiful service at the chapel in Aix En Provence where, at the crematorium, Arthur's ashes were placed in an urn to be subsequently carried with solemnity on board the Air France plane to Tripoli.

In the Libyan war cemetery under a cloudless sky, after some time searching for Ned's grave, Antoine, Betty, Ned and Aimee finally found it. As the hot sun beat down, they knelt and said their own special prayers for him, the soldier who died in the service of his country. Then they all stood, and Ben took a piece of paper from his pocket on which he had written the words of a poem, The Soldier by Rupert Brooke. Through misted eyes, he read:

If I should die think only this of me
That there's some corner of a foreign field that is forever England. There shall be
In that rich earth a richer dust concealed;
A dust whom England bore, shaped, made aware, gave once, her flowers to love, her ways to roam
A body of England's breathing air,
Washed by the rivers, blest by the suns of home.
And think, this heart, all evil shed away
A pulse in the eternal mind, no less
Gives somewhere back the thoughts by England given.
Her sights and sounds; dreams happy as the day.
And laughter, learnt of friends, and gentleness,
In hearts of peace, under an English heaven.

Wiping his eyes, he stuffed the paper back in his pocket. Then Betty opened the lid of the urn. She gently poured Arthur's ashes mixed with that modicum of England, the cow parsley, over Ned's grave to finally reunite her brother and father now both at peace in this foreign land.

Chapter Twenty-nine

It was Therese's wedding day, and it was probably going to be the hottest on record. The black crows were dropping out of the sky from the heat while the panting dogs lay listlessly under the trees.

Irene, Judy and Robert had all come over for the wedding. Robert had agreed with Irene that Therese's suggestion had been a good one. They were both not getting any younger and if the change would improve Judy's condition, then that would be all for the better. His house at Hove he had put on the market and had received quite a decent price for it. A young couple had bought it and planned to do some renovations, knocking out the wall in the kitchen and freshening up the bathroom. The furniture had been bought by a second- hand dealer who had been quite chuffed to obtain it as he had said there was a market for that particular style. Irene had thought he was welcome to it, old fashioned dust collectors that they were, she was glad to see the back of them. After all the selling had been completed, Robert had resigned from the Force, and been given a rowdy send off at the pub. It had taken a lot of self- control not to imbibe in anything stronger than lemon squash, so much beer and wine had been flowing, but to his credit he had come through unscathed.

Irene had agreed to Robert's marriage proposal and he had moved in with Irene and Judy until the forms were completed and their passages booked. Robert had the camp bed and Irene and Judy had squashed in together in Irene's bed. A day was set when Judy was in care, and they had gone to the registry office in London, there to be joined as husband and wife.

Mona was thrilled to have been able to witness the happy event as Rita had gone to look at alternative accommodation for them. They had also decided to move as they both could not forget the horrific sight of Mabel when they had discovered her dead in her room. Rita had even claimed that she saw Mabel's ghost one night on the stairs and had thought she had heard the piano being played when there was nobody about. It was not long after that the Rooms Vacant column in the newspaper was avidly perused.

Irene could not believe that she was now a married woman with a wedding band on her finger and could not stop looking at it for the rest of the day. They only had time for a quick bite at one of the Lyons Cafes as they had to be home in time to collect Judy from the centre. Robert promised that they would have a proper celebration when they arrived in Sydney. They were booked to stay at the Hotel Australia in Castlereagh Street for a few days before they made the trek to Therese's in Bourke, and Robert had heard that the hotel restaurant there was rather grand. After Robert had proposed to Irene, he had reassured her he would not expect her to give herself to him as a wife until she felt that she was ready. He was cognisant of the fact that she had never had a proper relationship up until now and he did not want her to feel pressured in any way. They would take one day at a time getting used to each other first. Irene had been so grateful that Robert had broached the subject as she had been loath to even mention it, so private and intimate it was.

The voyage over was similar to Therese's with many immigrants of different nationalities on board. Nearly all suffering from seasickness, they were however, excited about their futures in Australia. In between bouts of nausea, Irene and

Robert took turns looking after Judy who, strangely enough, seemed to come through the entire voyage unscathed. She delighted in sitting on the deck when all was calm, just looking at the sea churned white by the ship's propellers. And she was fascinated by the seagulls which swooped and dived over the ship, as they must have reminded her of the times spent at Brighton pier when she was with Irene and little Danny.

There were seagulls too, at Watson's Bay in Sydney. After they had checked into their hotel, they had taken a ferry from Circular Quay and eaten fish and chips at a cafe called Doyle's. It was owned by Alice who married Jack Doyle and they had opened a little tearoom at the beach in 1885. Watson's Bay had been a small fishing village populated with many Portuguese fishermen who had settled there many years before. From the cafe there was a beautiful view of the city which had Irene and Robert in awe. They thought it a charming place, and they could see Judy thought so too, as the seagulls flocked around her trying to steal the chips from her hand.

Afterwards, they all walked up through the park to the Gap which was a high cliff top place overlooking the ocean. They had been told by a couple at the cafe they it was a rather dangerous spot, as many people had ended their lives there by jumping over the edge, either drowning or landing on the rocks below. They walked along to where there was an anchor set into the stone. It was from the wreck of the Dunbar which foundered off the Gap in 1857 with 121 souls losing their lives. Irene had commented to Robert that thank goodness their ship had made the voyage safely with no such catastrophe occurring.

Another day, they took the train to Katoomba in the Blue Mountains and joined a coach tour. It was a day free of mist and, at Echo Point, they could see clearly the wondrous view before them - the majestic mountains: The Three Sisters, Mount Solitary and Narrow Neck all bathed in a blue hue. They were told by the tourist guide that the eucalyptus made the mountains look blue due to the vapour released by the trees. They took many photos with Irene's camera and then boarded the coach for a tour of Leura and Wentworth Falls where they alighted to see the three-tiered waterfalls thunderously cascading over the cliff. Judy had been mesmerised by this sight and had to be dragged away as the coach would have left without them. Irene always hoped that these new sights and sounds would stir something in her sister. Something that would give her back her speech, the speech which had been virtually non- existent for all these years. But still there was no sign.

Back at Katoomba, they were driven to a popular tourist attraction: the scenic railway. Irene was rather doubtful of riding in this contraption as she could see it plunged down a sheer cliff face to the bottom of the valley. They had been told that it had started off as a means to transport the coal up the cliff and, when the coal mine shut, it was turned into a tourist attraction.

After Robert's persuasion, Irene had eventually relented and they joined the other passengers in one of the most thrilling rides of their lives! It had not perturbed Judy. She had sat next to Irene and Robert and gazed about her as they were all plunged down the cliff face and then dragged back up. Irene had been pleased to alight, so anxious had she become that she had closed her eyes and hung on so tightly to Robert, she was sure he had left a mark on his arm.

After that adventure, a relaxing cup of tea was the order of the day, so the coach took them up Katoomba Street, depositing them at the Paragon Cafe. There they squeezed into one of the banquettes and ordered a Devonshire tea which reminded them of home and, on the way out, bought some Turkish delight and peanut brittle for which this cafe was famous. The day completed; they boarded the steam train which took them down the mountains back to Sydney.

Now, here they were in Bourke as Therese and Mick were to be joined together in marriage on the wide veranda of the homestead. To the relief of Irene and the assembly, as the sun sank behind the hills, there was a noticeable drop in temperature. Up until then, Irene has been concerned about the heat and worried if she would be able to withstand it if Brisbane was to be as hot. She remembered Therese saying that you could fry an egg on the ground in this country, it got so hot. She thought today she could do a good fry up with eggs and bacon and no mistake! Wiping her face with her handkerchief, she had whispered her concerns to Robert. He had squeezed her knee and reassured her that Brisbane would never be as hot as this, as it was near the coast, and not in the outback where they were now. Less concerned, she concentrated her attention towards Therese as she walked towards the priest. She looked beautiful dressed in a short cream satin dress purchased from a mail order catalogue and posted from Sydney. In deference to tradition, she had tied a blue ribbon around the top of her leg, and the something old was a brooch borrowed from Irene. In place of a veil, there was a garland of wildflowers adorning her auburn shining hair, which had been drawn up defining her jaw and exposing the white of her neck. In her hands she carried the same wildflowers as her bouquet. Her bridesmaid, Alinga, also carried wildflowers and she was dressed in an aqua satin dress also from the same catalogue. She had the widest grin which showed off her white teeth as she proudly followed the bride along the veranda to where Mick awaited. He was also looking resplendent in his mail order suit from Reuben F Scarf. He was going to wear the suit he wore to his father's funeral, but Dora would not countenance that! Wearing a suit of mourning to his wedding! No, he would be properly attired on this his special day and so a smart grey suit was ordered from Sydney, the account billed to Dora as a gift to her son.

Irene had charge of Danny who would not stop wriggling and tried to run after Therese as she was walking towards the priest. The priest, Father Ford, had travelled a long way to officiate at the wedding. However, he was used to travelling long distances to hold Mass in the isolated communities of this wide brown land. It was Judy who had stopped Danny in his tracks scooping him up and cuddling him, so pleased was she to have him in her arms again. Irene was pleased that she still remembered Danny as he had been just a tiny baby when last, she had seen him.

They were sitting with Mick's mother, Dora and her husband, Bill who had come from Broken Hill to attend the wedding. Dora was a plump country woman, the salt of the earth, and Therese had liked her the first moment they had met which was on their property at Broken Hill. Enveloping her in her big strong arms, she had told Therese she was so happy that Mick had found his true love at last and was besotted with little Danny, he now being her first grandchild. She had winked at Therese and told her not to wait too long to give Danny a brother or a sister so that they could be close and play together. She herself had been an only child and had found it quite a lonely existence, her mother being unable to conceive any more children after she was born.

Therese had enjoyed their journey to Broken Hill. It had taken six hours to travel there so they had elected to stay overnight on the property. They had driven through a similar landscape to Bourke, taking the Darling river route. The red river gums gave way to the vast ochre desert, dotted with spinifex, while overhead the wedge tail eagles soared high in the cloudless sky. As they travelled while Danny was asleep in her lap, thumb in his mouth, Mick had told Therese about the sheep station. His mother and Bill ran 6000 merino sheep on 600 acres and the wool was the highest quality being much in demand both here and overseas. He told her the shearing started in late spring, before the lambing season, the property abuzz with shearers clipping and sorting the wool. These shearers were itinerant workers, going from one property to the other during the season. He told her that in the days of the Depression there were men called swagmen who carried their meagre possessions in a "swag" over their shoulders walking the countryside seeking work. They used to help with the shearing and, if no permanent work was available, the farmer would provide them with food and shelter for some menial task. Therese thought what a class of a hard life it must have been then with no permanent home to live in. She looked down at her sleeping baby and then over at Mick. She counted her blessings that she had weathered her storm of adversity and would soon be settling down with this beautiful, caring man and living as a family on the homestead.

They drove on through the desert and soon passed a kangaroo with a joey in its pouch along the side of the road. Mick had then asked her had she heard of the Australian song, Waltzing Matilda? He explained that it had been written by a man called Banjo Paterson and was about an Australian swagman up to no good.

Therese replied that she had not heard of it and wanted Mick to sing it to her. So, after a little persuasion he relented, cleared his throat and sang:

Once a jolly swagman camped by a billabong
Under the shade of a coolabah tree
And he sang as he watched that jumbuck in his tuckerbag
You'll come a waltzing Matilda with me

This soon had Danny awake wondering what all the noise was about and Therese wondering who this jumbuck and Matilda were when they were at home?

It was not long until they had arrived at the property and, after lunch was eaten and they all had a rest, it was decided that they would drive Therese around to see the sights. Bill had completed the mustering by then and was also able to accompany them. They set off and, en route Bill had told Therese that in 1883, a boundary rider, Charles Rasp had come across what to him looked like tin but was actually silver and lead. It became the largest deposit of silver in the world and the Syndicate of Seven, men from the Mt Gipps Station, turned into The Broken Hill Property Company – BHP for short. Mick had previously told Therese that Bill was generally rather brief in conversation, but there was no stopping him when he was relating to strangers the history of his beloved Broken Hill.

The first place they went to see was the Line of Lode, a memorial erected to the 800 miners who had lost their lives mining the silver. It was erected high on a hill and commanded a superb view over the town. From there they had driven out to Mutawintji, where they witnessed numerous engravings of animals and animal tracks done by aborigines many centuries ago. Therese thought they were a bit like the drawings on the rocks in Bourke.

From there, they visited Sully's Emporium which housed Australian and European art as well as silver bracelets, earrings and rings. Therese had been drawn to a silver ring with a blue opal in the centre so Mick had purchased it for her, they both agreeing it would be their engagement ring. He had slipped it on her finger right there in the shop and they had sealed it with a kiss as Dora and Bill tried to prevent Danny's sticky fingers smudging the glass case.

Now Therese's finger sported two rings, the opal and the wedding ring. Under a canopy of multitudinous stars, there was a barbeque of fresh steaks and a pig roasting on the spit to feed the people. They had came from near and far to celebrate the marriage of farmer Mick, and the colleen from Ireland who had stolen his heart. Trestle tables covered with white sheets had been set up in the paddock, and it was on these tables that the food was placed. The wedding cake, a fruit cake laced with plenty of rum, was made by Dora. It was three tiered covered in white icing with pink roses piped around the edges. It had afforded her pleasure to make, and she had been pleased with the result. She was rather an expert in cake making and decorating, having entered her cakes in the Royal Easter Show. On one occasion she had brought home a blue ribbon, best in show in the fruit cake division! She had placed atop the wedding cake a little toy cow with two figures which were supposedly the bride and the groom. Therese thought it was charming and, after the cake had been cut by herself and Mick, Therese had given the cow to Danny who was more interested in licking the sweet icing than the toy itself.

Therese had been sorry that her parents were not there to share her special day but that was life. She fervently hoped that she would be forgiven and maybe one day she could take Danny back to Ireland. There was no way her mother would ever be able to make the trip out here. She really was not a one for the travelling. She had replied to her mother's last letter and insisted that no her Mick's eyes certainly were not close together and a more trustworthy man you could not find anywhere around. Not like that eejit who had relations with that sheep! She determined to write again to her mother and send the wedding photos so she could see for herself what a kind face her husband had. There were quite a few photos which had been taken with Irene's box brownie as well as Bob's more modern camera so there were plenty to go around. Bob had kindly taken on the role of best man as Mick's friend, Adam, had at the last minute, come down with glandular fever. With his gift of the gab, Bob's speech seemed to be interminable, with many references to Terry from Ireland and her bonza boy Danny, and hoping there would be many more patters of little feet about the place in the not too distant future. This had made Therese blush to the roots of her hair and it was to the Lord she had then begged forgiveness for disobeying her Mother once again, as she had slept with Mick before her wedding day. The first stirrings of pregnancy were emerging, and she hoped that everyone, and particularly her mother, would believe that the baby had been premature when it was finally born.

They had both succumbed to temptation the night Mick had proposed. As the last rays of the sun had disappeared over the horizon, and the last drops of wine had been consumed, Mick's proposal had been accepted. They had then sealed their commitment melding together on the rug, the chirruping crickets the only things to hear their joyous cries. After all passion was spent, Therese now knew the true meaning of the act of love. It was not that quick fumbling she had experienced with Dougal, but a consuming desire to be totally with another person. She had not yet told Mick her good news, but planned to tell him when they were alone together tonight in their official marital bed.

Everyone hoped that Bob's speech would wind up so that they could get on with the more important matters of dancing, singing and drinking. Mick had with the help of his mother and Bob, decorated the hay barn for the occasion. They had placed old glass jars, some containing candles and others containing wildflowers, here and there on the hay bales. The services of a local band called The Bourkos had also been obtained and, upon the conclusion of Bob's speech, they launched into a Hank Williams song "Hey Good Lookin'" which had the assembly up and dancing. This was the commencement of a long night of frivolity, and there were plenty of sore heads around the following day, testament to the many beers consumed. Irene and Robert had only drunk lemonade and they, as well as Judy seemed to be the only ones not suffering from "the morning after the night before" syndrome, much to their relief. Mick had insisted that people stay overnight, either in the homestead if there was room, or in the barn to avoid a long journey home in a state of inebriation. He knew that many country people drove while intoxicated and, although the local police turned a blind eye to the practice, Mick would never have forgiven himself if someone had died returning home from his wedding. He had heard of such a case a few months ago when a drunk driver had slammed into a road train, killing the driver and his passengers instantly.

Irene had felt so lucky to have Robert as her husband, so supportive was he ensuring that she always had a glass of soft drink in her hand. Mick had got along famously with the two of them, Therese ecstatic that her friend had finally married Robert and appeared to be as happy as she. Mick's sister, Maureen, had unfortunately been unable to attend the wedding as she had taken herself to Norfolk Island for the Christmas break. However, she had sent a telegram wishing her brother and Therese every happiness for their future, with a solemn promise to visit them before her pupils returned to school in January.

Mick had promised Therese that after they were married, she was going to have help with the household chores. He had laughingly told her she was now "the lady of the house" and as such would not be expected to be a dogsbody around the place. To her delight, she discovered her help would be none other than her friend, Alinga. Mick knew that Alinga was a good worker and trustworthy and he had seen the two of them had bonded well. Alinga had been thrilled to have been asked to help out missus and look after that Piccaninny Danny.

Irene and Robert were going to live in Greenslopes, a suburb in Brisbane. Robert had been fortunate to have secured a desk position in the Coorparoo Police Force, the next suburb away. Prior to emigrating from Britain, he had been finding work at his local station rather arduous now he was getting on a bit in years. The attendance at drunken brawls, domestic and otherwise, and having to inform parents of the deaths of their children after fatal road accidents, or drowning at the beach, had all taken their toll. Now he just wanted to sit at a desk, take it a little easier, and write reports, however mundane they proved to be. He had applied for such a job but there was nothing available. The only place which had an availability was at Hastings, but the commute was too long; over an hour by car or two hours by the bus. And that was just one way! He was looking forward to living in Brisbane and seeing one of his British friends who used to live in Chester. He was transferring to Brisbane as he had had enough of the weather in Melbourne. He had told Robert that it was nearly the same as living in England. Some days were as cold as charity! Hearing this, Robert had been thankful they had not nominated to live there!

It was the final day of their stay with Therese and Mick. Irene and Robert were putting the finishing touches to their packing. Closing their suitcases, they discerned through the window, Judy, sitting on the veranda completely mesmerised by what seemed like a large bird perched on the railing. It was looking down at her and then flew off to the nearest tree where it sat on one of the branches. They saw Judy following, and it was then that they heard the laughter. Firstly, from the kookaburra, then as the silence was drawn from her belly where it had resided up until now, Judy joined in the cacophony, the laughter bursting from her lips in a rusty trebled joy. It reached the ears of Irene and Robert who ran to her side. Judy had finally discovered her voice in this isolated place! At last, a kookaburra had given her back her voice!

“Kookaburra, kookaburra!” she cried.

“Yes dearest, it’s a kookaburra” Irene assured her, tears of happiness running down her cheeks. The three of them hugged and danced around in the dust all laughing and crying at the same time, while the bird flew away over the red hills. Arm in arm, they hurried back to the homestead, impatient to impart to everyone the wondrous news of the miracle which had just occurred in the red dust of this great southern land, Australia.

Epilogue

The London Times
January 19th 1952
The French ship Ile de France en route from Marseilles to Havana has foundered on the Jardines de la Reina 60 miles off the southern coast of Cuba. According to Cuban authorities there were 100 survivors and 50 missing, feared drowned. The ship was on its way from the port of Marseilles to Havana when it struck the reef in a violent storm. A search is now under way to locate any survivors.

The London Times
January 31st 1952
The body of a man has been found washed up on Varadero beach 87 miles from Havana in Cuba. It is thought to be one of the missing passengers from the ill- fated Ile de France ship which sunk off Cuba a few weeks ago. The man is a Caucasian and appears to have had undergone rhinoplasty surgery as there is a significant scar on the columella of the nose. No other identification was found, and the body has been transported to the city morgue in Havana for further forensic examination.

The London Times
February 15th 1952
A painting, The Water Lily Pond, thought to be an original by Claude Monet, was found washed up on Cayo Santa Maria beach 386 miles from Havana, Cuba. The painting, severely water

damaged was taken to the Museo National de Ballas Artes in Havana where authorities confirmed it to be a fake.

The Brighton Daily
July 18th 1960
The old brown lodging house on Brighton Boulevarde, known to locals as Mabel's house, was demolished yesterday to make way for a three- storey hotel to be built on the site. The lodging house gained some notoriety when the landlady, Mabel Dawson, was brutally murdered by a suspected serial killer who had rented a room there. The killer escaped justice, but it was thought that he was one of the passengers who drowned when the Ile de France foundered off the coast of Cuba in 1952. The sister of one of the lodgers had been initially charged for the murder but was later found innocent of the crime. The new managers of the hotel, Kevin Norton and Ben Wallis, told the Daily that Ben has a connection to the site as it was where his grandfather, Major Arthur Curtis, had lived happily there for many years after his discharge from the army. Major Curtis was wounded at Flanders in the Great War. His ashes were scattered in the Libyan war cemetery where his son is interred. The hotel is due to be completed in 1964.

About the Author

From an early age, Annette was encouraged to write and was awarded several prizes for English.

A native of Sydney, Australia, she published a short story at the age of twelve.

She remained passionate to her writing, but the demands of raising a family left no time for writing.

Now retired, Annette has reignited her passion and has written six books with the seventh nearing completion.

Her interest lies in novels set around the periods of the first and second world wars.

Annette lives with her partner, Stephen, at Neutral Bay, a suburb on Sydney harbor in Australia. She has two sons, Mark and Brett, two grandsons, Jaime and Flynn and a sister, Maree.

The Lodgers is her third published novel.

www.ingramcontent.com/pod-product-compliance
Lightning Source LLC
Chambersburg PA
CBHW022148240626
47153CB00007B/2558

* 9 7 8 1 7 3 6 7 2 1 8 1 0 *